REIKI VIBES

HEARTWARMING STORIES

T0090445

Order this book online at www.trafford.com
or email orders@trafford.com

Most Trafford titles are also available at major online book retailers.

Edited by Jinny Rodrigo.
Cover Design/Artwork by Tamara Robinson.
Photography by Jannie Laursen.

Note for Librarians: A cataloguing record for this book is available from Library and Archives Canada at www.collectionscanada.ca/amicus/index-e.html

Printed in Victoria, BC, Canada.

ISBN: 978-1-4251-8494-0

Our mission is to efficiently provide the world's finest, most comprehensive book publishing service, enabling every author to experience success. To find out how to publish your book, your way, and have it available worldwide, visit us online at www.trafford.com/10510

Trafford rev. 8/6/2009

www.trafford.com

North America & International
toll-free: 1 888 232 4444 (USA & Canada)
phone: 250 383 6864 ♦ fax: 812 355 4082

ACKNOWLEDGMENTS

WE WOULD LIKE to thank all of the contributing authors for sharing their Reiki stories. All are significant and play an important role in harnessing the power of storytelling to educate, connect and inspire others. We would also like to thank the broader Reiki community for the support and enthusiasm they have shown for this project. We love you all!

We would like to thank Jinny Rodrigo for her commitment to providing a pair of "editing" eyes and comic relief to any situation! We would also like to thank Tamara Robinson of Dream in Dimension Graphic Design. Your intuitive and creative approach to creating the look of Reiki Vibes has made the process unbelievably smooth and exciting. Thank you for helping us to create our big thoughts!

Finally, Tania would like to thank her Mom for being a glowing example of determination and unconditional love. "Your faith and trust in me is the motivating force behind my accomplishments and drive to succeed. Love you!" Infinite gratitude extended to her family, friends and the wonderful Reiki group that surrounds her – you are all amazing souls! Last but not least, Tania would like to thank her remarkable "partner-in-vibes", Tracy Lydiatt. You are a goddess of inspiration, love and positive energy and I am eternally grateful to have you in my life!

Tracy would like to thank her partner, Andreas for being endlessly patient, providing heaps of support, love and hugs. She would also like to tell her Mom how much she appreciates her leading example of compassion, laughter, strength and perseverance. Tracy would also like to bestow the biggest hug and infinite appreciation on Tania Bakas for being an incredible partner in developing this idea. I couldn't have imagined a better fit! Finally Tracy thanks her family and friends whose presence in her life has helped shape who she is today.

INTRODUCTION

This book began as a wild idea floated across a dinner table in 2006. We were enjoying a late summer evening, beautiful food, drink and company. We began to talk about Reiki and what it meant to us, how it had changed our lives and our continued journey in life with Reiki. Several impactful stories emerged about personal experiences we had had with either receiving Reiki or giving Reiki sessions to friends, family and clients. We both sat in awe and said:

"What would it be like to share stories like this with the world?"

"Maybe we should write a book?"

And thus Reiki Vibes - Heart Warming Stories was born!

We would like to take a moment to say the stories included in this book focus on Reiki as a complementary addition to any medical regime. Reiki is most often used as a stress reduction and relaxation technique. Reiki Practitioners do not diagnose conditions, do not prescribe substances or perform medical treatment, nor interfere with the treatment of licensed medical professionals. It is recommended that individuals see a licensed physician, or licensed health care professional for any physical or psychological ailment or condition they may have.

Reiki works with the body's ability to heal itself, and to do so complete relaxation is often beneficial. Long-term imbalances in the body can require multiple Reiki sessions to allow the body to reach the level of relaxation necessary to bring the system back into balance. Self-improvement requires commitment on the part of an individual, and they must be willing to change in a positive way if they are to receive the full benefit of Reiki.

We hope that you enjoy the stories we have collected and remember that a large, global community of Reiki practitioners and enthusiasts are continually contributing to the well-being of all life that is contained on our little planet!

Much love and light,
Tania Bakas and Tracy Lydiatt

CONTENTS

TANIA BAKAS AND TRACY LYDIATT

MY DAY AS A REIKI ANGEL
by Anne L.

MY STORY is about the power of Reiki and its ability to connect us with the Source and to each other.

I was spending an afternoon with a friend who is a fellow Reiki Master and we had walked into a shop that sells all kinds of rocks, crystals and semi-precious stone jewellery. As we were walking around the store, "oohhing" and "aaahing" over the items, I found a piece of amethyst that I just could not put down. I commented to one of the girls working at the shop that I felt I could not put the rock down. She laughed and pulled a rock out of her pocket and said that she had been carrying her piece around for several days.

She then began to tell my friend and I that she had been experiencing a major emotional release from her heart chakra and was feeling pretty drained and tired, unable to focus and just trying to get through the day. I felt much compassion for her so I offered to give her Reiki at which time, my friend also offered her Reiki services. The shop girl decided to take us up on the offer so the three of us retreated out behind the rock shop building and sat on a sunny bench right beside a duck pond.

As we were settling onto the bench, a small child came running over as he was chasing some of the ducks and geese. He was uttering this low guttural growl at the birds as he chased them and the shop girl burst into laughter and said, "I'm so connected to my environment. That kid sounds exactly like the feelings and emotions I've been releasing from my heart chakra!"

As we proceeded with our impromptu Reiki session, a deep sense of calm came over me and it was the most peaceful experience I had had for a long time. Working with another experienced

Reiki Master was an incredible experience as her hands would go to the places on the shop girl's body that I was going to next or we would put our hands on the same place of the body at the same time. It was beautiful.

I think we sat on the bench, in the sun, listening to the ducks in the pond, giving the shop girl Reiki for only ten or fifteen minutes. She looked like a different person afterwards and admitted that she was feeling much better and more focused. We closed the session, returned to the shop and continued looking around. When it was time to leave and make our purchases, she 'gifted' some of our items to say thank you for our Reiki contribution. It was such a surprise and a beautiful way of exchanging energy.

The shop girl shared with us that only one hour prior to our arrival she had silently asked her archangels for help and support for resolving her emotional release. She felt that we were sent to her as a direct reply from her archangels. What a beautiful day!

SILENT MESSAGES
by Sharon Storoschuk

I HAD BEEN PRACTICING REIKI FOR A WHILE when I received a phone call from a woman I did not know. Her name was Samantha and she wanted a Reiki session. When she arrived for the session, she told me she had never tried any kind of energy work before but felt drawn to Reiki. A Reiki practitioner who lived nearby had given Samantha my name.

Samantha and her husband had been trying for seven years to conceive a child but had no luck. They had tried almost everything and in a month's time, were scheduled for In Vitro Fertilization. Samantha felt this type of procedure was very invasive and the idea of the procedure had spurred feelings of reluctance in her. I think that somehow her body and the universe were telling her to try "energy work". Her first session was very intense and she was able to relax. I felt quite a bit of cold and emptiness in her solar plexus and sacrum area. After the session she was surprised at how much she had relaxed, as she was a self-identified, Type A personality.

Some time passed since the session when the phone rang one evening. It was Samantha. She was pregnant and ecstatic! We both could not believe it. It was a miracle.

She had a difficult time with the first three months and was quite nauseous, but that was bearable for the gift they had received! I am in awe of how the universe works and how our own bodies tell us what we need. When we put thoughts out into the universe, we get it! Thank you Universe!

BABY ADRIAN
by Tania Bakas

LITTLE ADRIAN, my friend's one year old son, was experiencing serious digestive problems. Although Adrian had a very healthy appetite and loved his food, shortly after eating he would vomit and never give himself a chance to hold in the nourishment of his mother's milk. He had seen many doctors and specialists, was on medication that was not working for him and the diagnoses were vague. The family was told that Adrian appeared to have an underdeveloped stomach and esophagus.

Just before his one year birthday Adrian was several pounds underweight, and was not quite as bouncy and giggly as usual.

I offered to go see Adrian and see if Reiki would help his situation.

He had just woken up from his nap when I went to visit the family's home and little Adrian was quite grumpy. Every time we would make eye contact he would start crying. He absolutely would not come near me. His mother tried repeatedly to bring him close by and he would start crying again. I told her I would just wait until he relaxed and I would let him approach me when he was ready. We waited half an hour before she could sit next to me with Adrian on her lap. He was resistant to me touching him so I sent him Reiki from about a foot away. I set the intention for the Reiki to flow to him if he was receptive to it, otherwise for the energy to be reflected into the Universe.

I had tried to explain Reiki to the Mother but there was a language barrier and it seemed that she did not fully understand. I wanted her to feel comfortable with me and perhaps then Adrian would warm up to me as well. I asked her to put her hand between my hands without having them touch. I wanted her to feel the energy without the physical contact. She immediately felt the warmth and tingling sensation and I saw her eyes lighten up. While I was flowing Reiki into her hand, Adrian had quietly slipped from her lap and was now lying between the two of us nibbling on a little biscuit. He was quiet and content.

I placed my hands over his tiny body, constantly adjusting my hand positions as he rolled around playfully. Soon he was playing on my lap and would smile at me every time I asked him if he felt better. I stayed with him for about an hour. Before I left I suggested to Juliette to connect with him when he is asleep, and send him thoughts of love, repeating the message to him that he is "safe" and surrounded by people that love him. I also suggested that when she is breastfeeding him to reinforce that her milk is good for him and that he is taking in life and all that is good for him. I showed her to hold Adrian close to her in such a way so that their heart chakras are connected and I explained that this will help him feel more connected to her and safe.

The next day I saw my friend, I asked him how little Adrian was feeling. With a big smile on his face he said that the baby boy's face did not look as pale anymore, his energy had increased and the vomiting reduced significantly. We made plans to visit him again a few days later.

On our second visit Adrian had so much energy that it was impossible to get my hands near him. He was bouncy, giggling and wanted to play. I sent Reiki to him from across the room while he played.

His Mother was in awe and could not believe her son's improvement. She was so grateful for this energy that came through my hands. I explained to her that we all have life force coming through us and that she too had a healing ability - especially for her son. I told her that I could help her "open" herself to the energy so that she too can help Adrian the way I did. With her permission, I attuned her to Reiki Level 1. During her attunement she said she felt her hands rising as if this energy from "above" was connecting to her. After the attunement I showed her how to feel the energy between her hands and it was immediate. She was so grateful that she kept kissing my hands, thanking me in tears. I suggested that she use her intuition to help Adrian, to place her hands over his little body when he slept or anytime he is receptive to it.

A few more days went by since my last visit with Adrian and I followed up with my friend to see how the boy was progressing. The father had tears in his eyes. Apparently Adrian had been eating and was now digesting his food with very few episodes of vomiting. His Mother had been giving him Reiki many times during the day and his improvement was impressive. Little Adrian does not experience any digestive problems anymore and is a healthy, bouncy little toddler.

RETURNING HOME
by Marianne Goetsch

IN SEPTEMBER OF 2000, I was called to Germany, as my uncle was in the hospital with prostate and bone cancer. Since he lived by himself, his doctor asked me to put him in a nursing home, but my uncle refused. Many years earlier when I lived in Germany, I had promised my uncle that if it came to this kind of situation, I would come and help him.

When I arrived in Germany, his doctor explained to me that they had operated on the prostate cancer, but could not do anything about the bone cancer and my uncle had refused chemotherapy and radiation treatments. He explained to me that my uncle would have maybe another two months to live but would likely not see Christmas that year. The doctor also told me that my uncle's liver was in a very weak state because of all the medication he had taken in the hospital. The same day I arrived, my uncle was released from the hospital into my care. He was only a third of his original weight, bedridden and very yellow in the face.

I stayed in Germany to take care of my uncle. I promised myself to do whatever was in my power to make his remaining days as good as possible. We changed all his medications for homeopathic ones, added minerals and vitamins, and cooked fresh meals every day with a lot of vegetables and fruit. I also talked with him about positive thinking and to help him in the healing process, I treated him with Reiki daily with friends sending distant Reiki too. Additionally, a physiotherapist came in once a week to work with his muscles.

We worked every day with Reiki and positive affirmations and one month later, his doctor came to visit us. My uncle was dressed and sitting in a chair. The doctor looked at my uncle, then at me and back and forth. He asked me, "What did you do?"

At first I thought maybe I had done something wrong, so I asked him, "Did I do something wrong?"

He came to me, shook my hand and said, "Whatever you're doing, keep on doing it!"

I stayed with my uncle in Germany for four months, and the cancer went into remission. Before I left, I checked my uncle into the hospital for a very good check-up. He had a clear bill of health. My uncle kept on living by himself in his apartment and enjoyed many more wonderful years. The cancer never came back.

We are so thankful for the gift of Reiki.

MY REIKI STORY
by Mia Rose

ONE DAY A CO-WORKER told me she was offering a Reiki work-shop and invited me to come along. I did not know much about it but for some time had been interested in the idea of hands on healing.

I went to the workshop and it felt very natural to me. I really embraced Reiki from the first moment but it took a long time for me to develop a deeper understanding and appreciation for the gift I was given that day.

After the workshop I recalled a meeting I had months before with an old psychic named Adele. She had told me I should become a healer as she held her hand above mine and I felt the energy flow between our palms.

Life had not been easy for me. A difficult childhood had set me up for an even more difficult adulthood. All the things that had happened in the past had left me on very shaky ground and with little idea of how to make it better. When I was twenty-three years old, my father died and I really lost the plot of my life. A few months after that, I fell for the charms of a cruel man who in turn almost destroyed me. Three years later when I had left him and was trying to put what little was left of myself back together again, I opened up to Reiki.

Reiki came along at the perfect time. I did not know it then but Reiki would precipitate some of the most profound, deep spiritual experiences of my life; both "good" and "bad". By learning how to help others, I also learnt how to help myself. Reiki guided me through.

My life now is so radically different from what it once was.

For the first time ever, I am truly happy. I give Reiki to myself, to others, to animals, to the earth and the Universe and I feel good. Reiki has added so much light to my life I cannot imagine going back into the dark.

REIKI FOUND ME
by Elizabeth Ann Candlish

MY STORY begins on my 50th birthday, when I was given a gift certificate for a facial and a hot rock massage. The facial was really good, but while the practitioner was doing the hot rock massage I also sensed and felt that she was doing something else, but I had no idea what.

When I came out of the room I asked the receptionist what the practitioner had been doing in addition to my massage as I could feel it. The receptionist informed me that she was doing Reiki during the hot rock session. I asked if anyone could do Reiki and she said yes.

It was amazing to me that I went into the salon feeling very stressed with the usual things on my mind; working in the week, shopping on weekends, chores, laundry etc. and I came out of the salon that day as if I was walking on air! I felt no stress, no weight on my shoulders, and I felt lighter and wonderful inside.

My interest was peaked and two months later, I had taken my Reiki Level 1. Now seven years later, I am a Reiki Master/Teacher and I have my own business with students and clients that also love Reiki. I am so pleased that the gift certificate was given to me and that Reiki came into my life. I had never even heard of Reiki before that day, but now I talk about Reiki to everyone.

What a life changing experience that was for me.

REIKI IN EVERYDAY LIFE
by Panna Majithia

REIKI is helping me with my everyday life. I have been a very emotional person, and in using Reiki every day, I have been able to become stronger and more positive in life.

With Reiki, I have been able to "let go" of many things. It is extremely powerful. I am also quite forgetful and when I misplace something and have difficulties finding it, I apply an appropriate Reiki symbol on my crown chakra and repeat that I want to find that particular thing in the next five minutes. And lo and behold, I find it!

When my day gets very stressful at work or I have backache or a headache, I give myself a quick Reiki treatment in the evening. I feel great afterwards. I use Reiki on myself almost every day. It helps not only heal my body but keeps me much more in touch with it.

I would recommend anyone with Reiki experience to explore self-healing on themselves. It helps one gain understanding of how Reiki works on others when you are aware of how it works on you. Reiki means everything to me!

HOW REIKI SAVED ME
by Juliette Sinclair

As a teenager, I suffered extreme pain from Endometriosis. For many years, at its height, three weeks out of every four I spent in bed. It was debilitating to say the least. I was missing 80% of high school classes, was struggling to keep my jobs and was prescribed copious amounts of heavy painkillers. During my worst days, I was barely aware of my surroundings.

On such a day, my mother telephoned a Reiki Master/Teacher she knew and arranged for an immediate healing session. Seven Reiki students were also called in to help. I had to be carried into the house of the Reiki Master/Teacher and all eight Reiki healers went straight to work with their hands resting inches above my body. Slowly I was able to communicate and was guided through powerful visualizations. The intense pain began to subside and finally disappeared completely; I went from a tightly curled foetal position to lying comfortably straight.

After a couple of hours I sat up pain free and noticed I was in her living room and began to introduce myself and thank them profusely. The Reiki Master/ Teacher told me she would send me distance healing in the future as well. As I was walked out the front door, her husband told me he was "now a believer" in his wife's healing abilities. There was no denying the change in my condition.

I never suffered such pain again and was inspired to follow my healer's footsteps. I began my Reiki training in 2004 and became a Master/Teacher myself. Now I can give back this precious gift to those in need. I am constantly finding ways to apply Reiki Energy to situations and witness the healing benefits take place. Not only healing body, mind and spirit but everything from preparing family meals; infusing them with Divine Love, to manifesting protection and the Highest Good in crisis situations.

My Faith rests in Reiki.

WONDERFUL RECOVERY
by Marianne Goetsch

SIX YEARS AGO, my friend was diagnosed with a tumour in her head, growing around the nerve (N.vestibulocochlearis) connecting to the brain stem (Truncus cerebri). Because of the pressure and dizziness she experienced, she agreed to an operation.

She had her Reiki Level 1 and she treated herself daily or I gave her Reiki sessions prior to the operation. After the operation, her son phoned me right away and asked me to come to the hospital. My friend was still in the recovery room so I went right away to the hospital and her son told me that the tumour was still in her head. After a twelve-hour operation, the surgeons gave up because the tumour had grown around the nerves and the damage would have been too severe if they removed it.

Right away I gave her Reiki. The next day we were told that they injured her voice box during the surgery so my friend was not able to talk to us. They had also damaged the oesophagus and she had to be fed through a tube, which was inserted in her chest. We gave her Reiki on a daily basis, sometimes more than one session a day.

Still today, she is a wonder for the doctors because after four weeks, her voice came back, and after four months, she asked the doctor, against their advice, to take the tube out and eat normally again. She has never had any further problem with the tumour either. The tumour stopped growing and it just sits there but does not cause any problems.

Reiki is the most wonderful gift we could ever receive.

HEALING OBSERVATIONS
by Julie Maher

MY NAME IS JULIE and I have been practicing Reiki for just less than four years now. I have to say that Reiki has had a profound effect on me and I have learned many a lesson over the last few years. Reiki is something that I want to share with everyone that I meet. I have a business now, practicing Reiki, and sometimes write about my experiences in a journal. I would like to share some of this with you.

Client: Mrs. MS (In remission / Lupus Chronic Back Pain)

My client had been heavily medicated for approximately two years and was in a stressful work situation. She had been suffering from a migraine headache for a week.

Our session lasted for one hour during which Mrs. MS and I experienced extreme heat for the first fifteen minutes of the treatment. Her pain started to shift from her head down into her neck. She had a lot of pain present in the back but it gradually settled and after the treatment, she reported just a slight headache and her back pain had eased a little. She planned to return the next day for a treatment and I gave her some lavender oil to put under her pillow while sleeping or on a handkerchief in her pocket during the day.

The following day Mrs. MS went to work and returned in the evening for another Reiki treatment. She reported she had a good day at work with just a very slight headache. She was able to cope well with it and in general, she was feeling much better in herself and had decided to have weekly Reiki treatments.

My observations from following Reiki treatments were that Mrs. MS had noticed a shift in her back pain. She was now able to handle stress at work by allowing herself to walk away from confrontation, and deciding she did not need to take on other peoples' problems. She was still having occasional days where she was apprehensive about going to work and when this would happen, we would have a couple of chats over the phone talking through fears and experiences. On a final note, she reduced her pain medication dramatically after approximately six Reiki treatments. We continue to have weekly Reiki treatments.

Client: Mr. DC (Enlarged right kidney)

Mr. DC used to drink large amounts of coffee. As a result, a previous inflammation flared up that blocked a tube and caused severe pain for my client. His doctor had prescribed anti- inflammatory medication as well as strong pain relief medication. Mr. DC had been taking the pain tablets and had hardly experienced any relief when he came to me for a Reiki treatment.

During our first Reiki treatment, Mr. DC was in severe pain during the session but the pain levels subsided after fifteen minutes of Reiki. We took a break and I gave him more Reiki one hour later. His pain levels continued to fluctuate during our session. Our second treatment lasted about thirty minutes. After which, I urged him to drink plenty of water and I returned to give him more Reiki that evening.

I had contacted a friend who also does Reiki and talked to her about what had happened earlier in the day. We arranged for her to send distant Reiki at the same time I would be giving Mr. DC his third Reiki treatment. He was in agony a couple of minutes into this treatment. He started shaking and questioned if one could have too much Reiki. I comforted him, assured him that it would be ok and asked if he wanted to continue. He said "yes" so we continued with the Reiki treatment. After thirty-five minutes, we had worked through the pain, taking breaks when needed and Mr. DC said he wanted to lie down and sleep. I was very relieved to see this as it is very hard to see someone in so much pain. The feelings I experienced while giving these treatments were so intense I find it hard to describe.

The next evening I returned to my brave client and was happy to see a dramatic improvement in his condition. He told me that not long after I left the previous evening had he passed small amounts of urine every few minutes for a couple of hours and he fell asleep about 11pm. The next morning he woke up to a small amount of pain but very happy with the remarkable improvement from previous days.

Our fourth Reiki treatment went for about forty-five minutes with pain moving around in the back area. I felt there was a lot of heat in the stomach area but overall, this area seemed much better for him than our previous sessions. We arranged to have ongoing Reiki sessions.

Throughout the following sessions, Mr. DC and I both experienced heat in the stomach and back areas. He mentioned feeling much improvement and was back at work with only small, niggling pains throughout the day. Towards the end of our sessions, Mr. DC was virtually pain free, which was a huge improvement from our first session. He told me he was still restless at night and was experiencing some headaches so I urged him to drink plenty of water to flush out toxins that were now unblocking and moving around. He described his night restlessness as a lot of thoughts and pictures going through his mind. During our sessions, he seemed to be relaxed and began sharing a lot of his thoughts. I felt he needed to let go of a lot of thoughts in his head so I gave him a meditation CD to listen to. I felt it would help him get his head around a lot of the thoughts he was dealing with. He said that he felt a lot better in himself now.

This is just a sample of what I have experienced during treatments. I know this is just the start of what is to come. Reiki is my life now and I hope to touch many lives with the gift that I have been given.

DON'T QUIT FIVE MINUTES BEFORE THE MIRACLE

by Lyn Elizabeth Ayre, Ph. D

FOR ME, Reiki means health and well-being. I had been very ill for a very long time being diagnosed with Lupus and Multiple Sclerosis (MS). In addition, I had several subsequent medical diagnoses, experienced a variety of devastating neurological symptoms that resulted in the loss of my mobility and I eventually found myself in an electric scooter, used a wheelchair for malls and hospitals, and canes for around the house. My thoughts, energy, sexuality, speech, employability, and most of all, my peace of mind, were all affected by these illnesses.

For about a month during the spring of 2002, I had been praying several times throughout the day for God's healing grace to enter me and restore my health and mental clarity. As each day passed, I became more and more willing to change my thinking and let go of old outworn ideas and ideals. I felt a change begin to occur within me.

At the time, I was teaching a meditation course in a place which happened to display business cards and brochures of other practitioners. One night, I picked one up and read the word "Reiki". Something struck a chord in me. I recalled going to a two-day workshop with my boyfriend back in 1985 where a man was teaching about healing without touching. At the time, he did not impress me, as he seemed like a real money grabber. I had been doing hands-on-healing all my life and nothing he said made sense to me. It may have been Reiki and I just was not ready for it. I called the woman on the business card and made an appointment for the following week.

About halfway through the session, I began to giggle. I had opened my eyes and saw a beautiful gold and green light emerging from her head and heart, which was now hovering over me. It was at that point that I made the association that God's healing grace was working in my life – literally. My practitioner's name was Grace.

I spoke with her after and shared what I saw and the connection I made. I wanted to learn how to do what she was doing and make people feel the way she made me feel. We made an appointment for the following week. She gave me the Power Symbol that day and told me how to use it. On our appointment day, she spent some time going over the history, hand positions, and self-healing. She gave me another full-body session and then performed the four attunements for Level One Usui Reiki on me.

As the energy worked its way up through my chakra system, I experienced many things from severe diarrhoea to euphoria. Throughout those three detoxifying weeks, I felt on top of the world. I knew changes were being brought about in me by God but at the time, I had no idea to what extent. I just kept being willing to allow the changes, whatever they were.

A few days later, it was Father's Day and we had my family in for dinner. My sister brought a bowl of strawberries for dessert. I usually have only a tiny slice, refraining from eating them lest my mouth and throat break out in canker sores. No bumps appeared in my mouth. I made mention of this and took another strawberry – still no problem. My husband warned me against pressing my luck. I had another strawberry. In the end, I ate my portion and several others to boot! I was in heaven. The next day, I drank orange juice and ate tomatoes with no allergic reaction. I was floored. I knew it was Spirit's Reiki energy working another miracle in my life.

The swelling in my joints started to go down to the extent that I was able to start a weight training program and do interpretive dance to the music of Pachelbel. My eating habits began to change naturally. In addition to the above mentioned strawberries, orange juice and tomatoes, I added blueberries, cranberries, arugula, grapes, salad greens, and baby spinach – most of which I would not have touched with a ten-foot-pole prior to this point.

Some days, I would forget to take my medications and still feel okay. This was a true blessing. My energy had returned and I would get up at 6:00 a.m. to do my prayers and meditation. Then I would do a full-body self-healing and some reading, after which I would be ready to start my day. I had very little need for naps anymore but would take one if I needed to. When I went to bed at night, I did not feel exhausted and in pain. Instead I would feel wonderful and have a restful night's sleep.

Garbled thinking slowly vanished – it has been a while since I tried to put the milk in the coat closet. I would not forget why I walked into a room. I could remember everyone's name and the name of all the objects I would encounter in my daily routine. My dream life became very vivid and pointed. I learned many lessons while analyzing my dreams and writing them down became an important part of my growth.

I received the Level Two attunement in Usui Reiki three weeks after my Level One attunement. I experienced what is known as a healing challenge, where the symptoms are exacerbated to an extreme degree. It was my chance to have one last look at the diseases in my body and, once and for all, let them go to God. I have not had any significant Lupus or MS symptoms in several years.

I went through a bout of Trigeminal Neuralgia and twice-daily Reiki sessions kept the pain levels to the point where I could still enjoy my day. After my second attunement, I was able to let go of all the pain medications and cut the Lupus medications in half. My goal was to gradually let go of all Lupus medications over the next few months. I was successful and have now been off all medications for a few years.

REIKI IN ACTION - ADAM'S STORY

by Isabella Ferguson

"BE KIND WHENEVER POSSIBLE. IT IS ALWAYS POSSIBLE."

- DALAI LAMA

IMAGINE if you will a young, enthusiastic man in his mid 40's with two children and a wife who is his best friend. He is a musician skilled in both piano and guitar, a knowledgeable ornithologist, a vibrant lover of travel and camping, bouncing with energy and full of life. Suddenly one day, without warning, this young man experiences a catastrophic stroke. A frantic transport to the hospital and a new drug quickly administered in the wake of the emergency saves the life of this man but leaves him forever changed.

From one breath to the next, Adam's life became one of basic survival. After a period of hospitalization and physical therapy, Adam went home. His mobility was limited, he had trouble speaking, had forgotten most of his vocabulary, had little energy, and needed to relearn the basic tasks of daily life. At first, it was difficult, if not at times almost impossible, to communicate verbally with Adam and his fatigue precluded all but very short visits. It was distressing to see the terrible toll this event had taken on Adam, his family and friends.

We are a small community and try as best we can to support each other in times of crisis. This can take the very important form of practical matters, such as filling freezers with prepared meals, helping with gardening and chores, and offering rides when needed. All are blessed acts of kindness in themselves. I am fortunate to belong to a meditation group, which includes a number of Reiki Masters, and it seemed clear that the gentle, healing energy of Reiki would have much to offer to, not only Adam, but also his grieving family as they struggled to come to terms with their new reality.

On approaching Bev, Adam's wife, she was open-minded and grateful for the offer of support. A few quick telephone calls and we had a core of Reiki folks ready to do what they could to help. So it became the routine that every Sunday afternoon a number of us headed out towards the tranquil area in which the family lived. Greeting each other and the family with warm hugs we clasped hands to balance our energies and, with Adam stretched out on the dining room table, would begin to channel unconditional, compassionate energy. In addition to Bev and her best friend Cate, Dana and Evan, Bev and Adam's children, also became curious and soon we had two enthusiastic young recruits, eager to participate in this loving connection to their father.

Week after week Adam would be saturated with Reiki energy, warm palms of loving hands, sometimes so many passing the gift of this healing touch that we would channel Reiki to Adam through each other as we ran out of body space to hold! Laughter and tears would punctuate periods of incredible peace and stillness as we did our best to support the family on this challenging journey. Adam's courage and dignity were an inspiring lesson to us all.

As the weeks passed and fall flowers gave way to sprinkles of snowflakes we continued our sessions. Adam greatly looked forward to the variety of personalities who would arrive to work with him each Sunday and slept well after our sessions. As he dozed peacefully after treatments we would congregate nearby and discuss life, spirituality, recovery, the insights becoming clearer as we worked together. These times were not sombre but infused with lively discussion, shared stories, experiences of past lives together, many jokes and lots of tea! Although we could not reverse the physical damage done by the stroke we began to effect emotional healing and to feel the miracle of new friendships based on our spiritual connections. As the family worked to understand and accept the way things were now, all had a desire to be attuned to the Reiki energy. It became time to move to the next level.

In November 1999, five "new" practitioners were attuned to Reiki Level 1. Bev, Dana, Evan, Cate and Adam himself had deep understanding of the true heart of Reiki and together we worked through the other information they needed to know. Gradually they took over the healing themselves, Adam's life changed again as care aides came into his home on a daily basis, and Bev returned to part time work. Bev and Cate followed their spiritual path, joining our open and accepting group and embracing new ideas and approaches. We keep learning together.

The years have passed and the children have left home. Dana, Bev and Adam's daughter, has finished a course of study and entered the work field. She credits her Reiki background providing strength to her in times of need. Their son, Evan is busy being a teenage lad and we know his powerful connection to Reiki will be there when he calls upon it. Both youngsters were confident participants in a large Reiki share held locally some time ago. Bev has now been a long time member of our meditation and Reiki group and can often be found with us at a hospital bedside or offering healing energy to someone in need. Bev, Dana and Cate all went on to complete Reiki Level 2 training.

Adam himself is now a resident of a care home and his indomitable spirit is a source of enjoyment to those around him. Time moves on.

Those hours spent with Adam and his family were unique. Over the years I have found Reiki to be a most blessed gift, especially when serious illness presents itself. What could be more rewarding than sitting by the bedside of another in peace and quiet,

A LOSS AND SOME TO GAIN
by Andrea Bell

WHEN I FOUND OUT I WAS PREGNANT, there was an emotional space that was not yet filled with anything, and I did not know how to react or what to think. As time went by, moment-by-moment, that empty emotional space came to be filled with an excited joy that I had yet to know in my life. A new path started flashing before me, a stability, a grounding, a love, which I have never known before. Day by day, this grew into something that I could really relate with, something that seemed real.

About a week after I found out that I was pregnant, I started spotting. It appeared to be nothing serious, but I kept an eye on it as a possible issue. This kept on going until the day that I was booked for my first ultrasound. On the day of the ultrasound, the spotting turned into heavy bleeding, and in my case, became a miscarriage, crushing my ever so vivid dream.

I had completed Reiki Level 1 training in the past, and am blessed with the magical energy, so of course I spent quite a bit of time beaming lots of love at the little foetus growing inside of me. But, of course, as I have been reassured, there was nothing that I could do, and it was nothing I did, the pregnancy just was not right. It was rough at first and I felt as if I wanted to die and actually had visions of throwing myself in front of a bus, or pulling the ever so famous jumping off a bridge!

I had been putting off doing Reiki Level 2 for a little while and decided that this was the very best time to continue with my Reiki training. I am also blessed to have a wonderful and close friend, Tania, who is a Reiki Master, I found myself lucky enough to do my Reiki Level 1 training with her, and she offered Level 2 training. So, we set a date to do my Level 2 training.

I have found that attunements have been a wonderful experience. For me, the attunements are almost a psychic time where I see things that would never come at another time. What I will do with my life, how my life will end up, colours, shapes, love, and movement. It all comes rushing in during those moments. We did the attunement and a peace came over me, one that I had not felt since I found out that I had miscarried. As we continued throughout the day, I found myself letting things go and allowing the unspoken feeling to wash away. I allowed myself to say those unspoken things without such a heavy heart and I found myself smiling again, from the inside.

Becoming attuned to Reiki Level 2 was an amazing feeling. Not only did I feel the energy, I had the experience of seeing how Reiki can help initiate change, how it can truly heal, and how it can fill you, another, and the Universe with exactly what is needed when it is needed.

After my Level 2 training was completed and I had learned the symbols, I told Tania that I needed a release as I still felt heavy and that I felt it would help me if she did some work on my uterine area. So, I lay down on the bed, closed my eyes, and felt heat on my belly -not from the Reiki which was present but not yet flowing towards me- but from crystals. She had laid out an array of crystals on my pelvis; rose quartz, tourmaline, and many more. They were already giving off heat and filling the void there with something much needed: healing energy. Then came the Reiki, hot this time, and so very, very soothing. The empty space there seemed to be part of me again and I felt healed; mind, body, and spirit.

Since that day, I am able to speak of the loss, speak of how it has changed me and my life, and how to look forward with a smile again, rather than the feeling that everything is wrong. So many women go through similar experiences and it was by far the hardest loss I have ever dealt with in my life. A woman can so quickly become so attached, and then can so quickly lose it all. The pregnancy gave me a reason, a drive, and a new confidence that was not even close to being present before.

After losing the baby, I lost those feelings but am now able to look at it as an experience, which is not the end of me. I am now able to move on and know that I can have the life that I dream of, and that the love of a child will come, when it is the right time.

I will always have Reiki and it will continue to be warmth, love, and a healing power that I can share with myself and someday with others. It's something I feel truly blessed to have received and continue to share!

RECOVERING WITH REIKI
by Elfina Luk

A FRIEND OF MINE, who had been in a terrible car accident, was subsequently in rehabilitation at the GF Strong Centre in Vancouver, a hospital dedicated to spinal cord injuries. He only had feeling in his head, a bit down to the middle of his ribs, some in his left arm and only pain sensations in his left hand.

During one of our visits I asked if I could do some Reiki on him. At first I did some Reiki on the back of his neck where the injury occurred and he could quickly feel the intense heat coming out of my hand. Then I moved to his left hand and it was here where his expression changed. He looked perplexed. He said he could feel the heat from my hand; I nodded and continued with the Reiki. His facial expression was priceless as he was so astounded by the feeling of the heat, and it was then that I realized that this was the first time that he was able to feel heat in his hand since his accident.

After my visit, I felt he was another step closer in his recovery. Although it was a small step, it was nevertheless an amazing one for the heart and spirit. I have great faith that Reiki will shed a positive light on his journey to a speedy recovery so he can walk again.

I am so joyful and grateful that I was able to use Reiki to help him in this way. These are the moments I live for and one of the reasons Reiki is so important to me and inspires me to keep on doing what I'm doing.

REIKI
SUPPORT TO THE RESCUE
by Bobbi Casey

IN OCTOBER 2005, I entered the hospital to have a reversal operation. It was quite serious and the days following the procedure, I was on all sorts of machines to keep me alive, and I had picked up a superbug that was resistant to medication and did not help my progress healing. My Reiki teacher/friend Barb Weston came to visit me in the hospital and noticed how uncomfortable I was. I had taken my Reiki Level 3 by then and she decided to give me my Master attunements right there in order to assist my healing process. That night after the attunements were finished, I did a lot of self-healing on myself using Reiki energy.

The next morning when I awoke I noticed a lot of the swelling had gone down and the hospital staff had removed some of the tubes that were feeding me some of the medicines. All my vitals were normal so I phoned Barb immediately. She was very excited to learn that by my doing extensive Reiki on myself the night before, my medications were reduced and I was feeling noticeably better. I had been in the hospital for over a week but from that day on I rapidly improved.

MY FALL
by Pat Sweet

AT THE TIME THIS EVENT HAPPENED I was trained in Level 2 Reiki. I was getting a heavy platter from the bottom of a cupboard when I got careless and I felt a terrible pain explode in my back, causing me to collapse on the floor, whimpering. It hurt to move but because I live alone, staying put on the stone floor was not a good option. I decided if I could get upright and to a chair, I could do some Reiki and at least relieve the pain enough to think clearly.

I dragged myself up against the cabinets and found I could not walk. My left leg just would not work. I managed to walk/drag myself around to a chair and sat down. I was not being brave, only convinced giving myself some Reiki would sort out the problem. Once seated safely, I started Reiki on my back. What utter bliss! I could feel it absolutely walloping the pain away. I just kept running Reiki, even when I went to bed. Additionally, I asked my Reiki Guides for Reiki to run overnight and thankfully, I slept!

The next morning I did take one strong pain-killing tablet and when I saw the doctor, she said I had a prolapsed disc and trapped tendon. She sent me to physiotherapy and I went happily, grateful that the damage was not worse. I cannot take anti-inflammatory drugs due to a food/substance allergy but I can truly say I felt I did not need them, or the painkillers for that matter. I only missed eight days from work, six of which were physiotherapy days. In addition to the Physiotherapy, I called a Reiki practitioner who came round and gave me additional Reiki treatments.

I was fascinated to realise the Reiki took away most but not all of the pain, which was clever because that meant I couldn't get careless and over exert myself. I missed very little work hours and I did not miss any sleep, healing fairly rapidly despite being over 50!

MY GOOD HANDS
by Norman Ayre

Over the past 17 years, I have been exposed to many spiritual and holistic practices. Most significant among them was during a time when my wife, Lyn, was grieving her mother's death, and her spiritual mentor's passing, while at the same time dealing with the symptoms of Multiple Sclerosis and Lupus. I began attending Therapeutic Touch and Meditation sessions with her at a local hospital and immediately noticed a dramatic improvement in my attitude in the way I dealt with people. I could sense an opening in my heart centre.

I wanted to give back what I had received, so I began taking Therapeutic Touch and reading a wide array of spiritual books. I was told I had "good hands". When I practiced using my newfound abilities, people said they felt better afterward.

Shortly after becoming attuned to Reiki, I went on my first Shamanic weekend. I found this fascinating experience opened me up to new horizons and energies in healing. I have pursued this path, studying and taking courses as they came to my attention. I offer these practices for the benefit and growth of my clients.

Several years ago, I contracted an infection in my lower spine causing extreme pain and resulted in being hospitalised for a month. During this period I came to value Reiki more than ever. Even though I was on high doses of sustained release morphine I was still in pain. I would start channelling Reiki and this would result in a lowering of the pain level (Notice I did not say my pain level. Never own a disease or pain). I was also receiving distant Reiki from a small army of friends and their friends, so as I focused on the Reiki energy being sent to me the pain would subside, affording me hours of relative comfort.

Medical professionals had forecast 4 to 6 months to overcome this situation. I was back at work in ten weeks. I am convinced that it was the Reiki and my shamanic practices that helped me recover at this accelerated pace.

I continue to do my daily self-healing and other holistic practices as I am determined to regenerate the discs that the infection destroyed.

BRINGING
BALANCE WITH REIKI
by Anne L.

I HAD DECIDED to review my eating habits and had a live blood analysis done to give me a good inside view of what was going on in my body. I had never really had any serious health issues, just minor ones like fuzzy thinking, fatigue, small skin rashes here and there. My blood analysis revealed that I was quite acidic and on the path to developing more serious health issues in the future, namely high blood pressure and diabetes.

Right away, I decided that I would make a change in my eating and began to slowly transition my diet to include more alkaline foods and phase out white flour, sugar and dairy. Through reading about pH balancing in your body, I learned that stress can dramatically affect your pH levels but I did not really believe it until by chance, I managed to prove to myself that it was true.

I had booked a Reiki appointment (my first one in about 8 months) one day after work. So, when I arrived home, I had a glass of water and tested my pH with a pH strip for the second time that day. The strip's color told me my pH was about 6.0 (7.4 is alkaline) and I was confused because I had eaten only alkaline foods throughout the day. I left for my Reiki session and I had one of the most relaxing one and a half hours I had had in the last eight months.

When I arrived back home again, I thought it would be interesting to test my pH again to see if the Reiki had made any difference. Not expecting much of a change from the last test, I was shocked to see the pH strip register a pH level of 8.0 (or above) as the strip had turned a darker color than the color for level 8.0! I was amazed and totally surprised.

It reminded me how important it was to take care of my health and that I had been neglecting my energy needs. I have since booked regular sessions and will continue to monitor my pH levels before and after my Reiki sessions.

A REIKI STORY
by Ann Mayo

It was only about fifteen years ago that I was introduced to Reiki, and the more I learned about it, the more I realized that I had been using Reiki even as a child. Back then I did not understand why my hands and feet often got so unbearably hot and why I 'saw' things. I especially remember the beautiful colours.

It was my friend, Grace, who sensed I had a special "ability" and brought me to a Reiki group. That was the start of a beautiful and joyous journey, having the awareness of Reiki in my life.

About twenty years ago my dear friend, Andie was diagnosed with cancer. Many surgeries removed parts of her stomach, lungs, bowel and colon. Other surgeries removed her breasts and lymph system. Eventually the cancer clinic told her that the only thing she could do was to go home and wait to die.

Andie was a fighter and opted to see a naturopathic doctor in Vancouver. When she came down for treatments she stayed with me. We knew she did not have much longer on this Earth, and despite laughter there were many tears. I often encouraged her to think seriously about returning home to Australia as I thought it would be appropriate for her to die at home.

During our long conversations I told her about Reiki. She had heard of it but didn't know much about it. I did some treatments just on her head, and she loved the feeling it gave her. Then the magic happened. We were lying in bed one night when my hand needed to touch her armpit. It did not make any sense to me, so I asked her if it would be okay. Of course she agreed.

After about five minutes I felt a huge mass in my hand. It was about the size of a large grapefruit, and I 'saw' that it was black and covered with bristle-like thorns. Simultaneously we both said, "Wow!" then Andie began to cry. I was so very distressed about this until she told me why. Seven years earlier her lymph glands were removed, and as a result she had no feeling in her upper arms and armpits. She had to shave her armpits by watching in the mirror to make sure she did not cut herself. Suddenly after I gave her Reiki, all sensation had returned.

We got up, lit a few candles, drank some wine and laughed and cried until early into the morning. Andie continued to touch her armpits and marvel at the returned sensation after years of being 'numb'.

That was my last visit with Andie. Five days later she was on the plane home to Australia. By the time she got off the plane her legs were paralyzed, but she was at home with her family. A week later she left us to join the angels.

I thank God constantly for the magnificent gift He has bestowed on me. I think endlessly that if more people learned about Reiki, and if we all used our Reiki energy to heal this weary planet, what a lovely place it could be again.

Personal Growth & Development

MY PATH TO REIKI
By Susan Hollingshead

In 2002, I knew nothing about Reiki (not even the name). Things started happening to me; dreams, silent pushes etc. and then a book appeared on my bookshelf, "The Messengers, a True Story of Angelic Presences in this Day and Age" by Julia Ingram. I read it. Incidentally, the book makes no reference to Reiki at all. One morning I woke up and told my husband, "I am going to get my Reiki!" He asked me what it was, to which I replied, "I haven't got a clue!" That day, I went online and started to research Reiki. I found a Master in my area who, as it turned out was the wife of an old hairdresser I used to go to.

She arranged a class with one other girl. When I was attuned, my entire body began to vibrate like nothing I have ever experienced. It was the most amazing thing. I began having extraordinary dreams; I could not sleep more than four hours at night. People crossed my path who I had never met before, yet had always been right there under my nose; people who were very spiritual and who I have since become very close with.

My life has changed dramatically and my view of the world has too. I feel more compassion towards others and look for the positive sides in all situations. Prior to Reiki, I kept my beliefs to myself and now I share what I have learned with others. Though I am not religious (never was), I feel I know my Creator intimately now. I believe I was directed to Reiki to facilitate that.

I have had several encounters with departed souls while I have given Reiki treatments to my clients and I intuitively know where their problems are. I have helped others connect to their Creator as a result. One woman I worked with came to me for help as she was suffering with breast cancer for the third time. I sensed I could only help her to become less afraid and be prepared for what was to come. She came weekly for months and changed from a fearful, angry woman into a loving, peaceful one who felt self-love for the first time in her life. When I moved away, she continued to see my friend, a spiritual native healer, regularly as well. She passed away peacefully last spring. She was ready to go without suffering and her previously estranged children were at her side.

ALL ABOUT REIKI
by Julie Maher

REIKI to me is a way of life. It is about living something special and growing with that.

It teaches you such things such as trust, love, peace, and compassion. It helps you to accept what is happening in your life, without being judgmental. It allows you to detach from things that really are not your concern. We need to realize that everyone has a path already set out for them and they can grow and learn as they walk along this path. It is ok to be supportive of our loved ones, as they take this journey, but do not forget that we are on a journey too and we need to be mindful of our needs.

I love to watch as those with Reiki in their lives allow for change to happen. Sometimes it is very subtle at first, without them even noticing. Often it is the people around them who first start to notice the difference. When changes are taking place, growth is occurring.

When you are able to follow your inner feelings and just allow life to happen, you have a sense of inner peace. I now see that the simple things in life are also the most important things in life.

When we experience pain and illness, our bodies are bringing to our attention the need to stop and observe what is happening in our lives, or has happened in the past that we need to deal with. Breathe into it, feel it.

What do you see? What do you feel?

Reiki gives you strength to make decisions. Perhaps deep down you have always known what you would like to do, where you would like to go, whom you would like to be with, but you did not have the strength then to carry out these wishes.

Some times when we are hurting we think that Reiki is not working for us, but we have to understand that the outcome is not always going to be what we want it to be. Here is where the trust bit comes in. It is how you deal with whatever is put before you. Do not get angry, or feel sorry for yourself or others. Try looking at it in a different way. Learn from it.

Learn how to say no without feeling guilty. Just say it and let go. Walk away. Grieve without feeling angry. Many lessons we have to learn in life do not have to have all the added emotions like anger, frustration, sorrow, fear, and guilt. Look at it differently and see how it makes you feel inside. Feels good, doesn't it?

Sharing the special gift of Reiki with others gives a sense of absolute satisfaction I have not known before. The compassion that goes hand in hand with Reiki is something that I truly would love to see everyone share in their lifetime.

Sometimes it is at the end of life when Reiki is first experienced. What an honour to be able to give someone a true sense of inner peace to allow them to go from this stage of life to the next with joy and love in their hearts. For loved ones to see the peace they too can let go and allow a beautiful transition to take place.

REIKI "HELPERS"
by Susan Hollingshead

I HAVE HAD SEVERAL EXPERIENCES of being contacted by spirits who have crossed over when I have been working with clients. My challenge has been learning to "remove my thoughts and interpretations" from the process.

The following are some of the most memorable ones. The first time it happened was in 2003 when I was giving my late husband's mom a Reiki treatment on the tenth anniversary of his death. She was seventy years young then. Just after I laid my hands on her, I closed my eyes and immediately saw a "floating face" wearing a Fedora (at the time I didn't know what a Fedora was but the word came to me). This face also had a neck with a high shirt collar and even though I had never interrupted a session before to speak, I was compelled to ask her if her father ever wore a Fedora, which she confirmed.

I closed my eyes again and this man had removed his hat and was now "standing" at the end of the table. He had removed his jacket and vest to reveal a pair of suspenders and he had rolled up the sleeves of his shirt. He stayed there working with me for the duration of the session. As I was nearing the end of an hour, I saw him as part of a trio; he on one side, my late husband on the other side and her recently departed husband in the middle. I "sensed' her father and her son were there to help her husband become familiarized with his "new" residence. Needless to say this was very emotional for both of us.

Afterwards she went into her den and pulled out a photograph of her long departed father wearing a Fedora and a suit with "braces". It was the man who came before me during the Reiki session and I "felt" he was there to let her know he loved her. He was always with her and all her loved ones were together, even though her father had never met her husband on the earth plain.

I had another experience with spirits while I was working on the elderly wife of one of my regular clients. As I started to work, I closed my eyes and I saw a woman in a WWI nurses uniform, complete with the headgear of the period, an apron and mid-calf length dress. She hung around for a while and showed me herself working in a muddy field hospital (a large tent Operating Room) with poor lighting and chaos around her. She then showed me beautiful flora, fauna and waterfalls I just "knew" to be in Hawaii. I didn't interrupt my session this time but continued to work, sensing this nurse's presence the whole time. Afterwards I discussed my "vision" with my elderly client and she became very excited. It seemed our visitor was her adoptive grandmother, a nurse who during WWI had worked in horrible conditions in the field and who was now buried in Hawaii at the foot of a beautiful waterfall.

I was giving a treatment to a young, dark-skinned male client from the Philippines and soon after I laid my hands on him, I saw a very 'white' skinned Oriental woman I sensed to be in her early thirties. She just seemed to beam love for this man. I thought I "heard" her say her name was "Garanna".

Suddenly I felt like there was a vice around my heart and I almost stopped working but continued, knowing this was not my ailment I was feeling. Again, I just felt enormous love for this gentle man on my table. Afterwards, I discussed with him what I had experienced. Tears filled his eyes as he told me his mother was a fair-skinned Chinese woman named "Arhanna", who died very suddenly of a heart attack at the age of thirty when he was only three years old! I was able to convey to him how much she loved him and that she was always there, watching over him.

I feel I am truly blessed to have my client's departed loved ones connect to them through me. It is an ability that has come to me since I became attuned to Reiki and one I am forever grateful for.

WHY I WANTED TO BECOME A REIKI MASTER/TEACHER

by Veronica Hanegraaf

EVER SINCE I WAS A YOUNG GIRL, I felt I was different, not special, but just different. I tried to fit the narrow box others confined me to but it never really worked. I was a people pleaser. I wanted people to like me. I could always see both sides of a story or argument so my friends started calling me "Miss Swiss" because I was neutral and would not take sides. This has helped me become good at being a mediator and a great listener who has no judgment.

I was always a happy child, filled with light and laughter but there were emotional and sexual abuse incidents which stole my light for a time. I have always had a journal and poetry writing plus other creative outlets to help me through these life experiences. For the past twenty years, I have been working on my issues, the main ones being low self-esteem and self-worth, through many different modalities. I have had art therapy, Shamanic Counselling sessions, Reiki, EFT, Crystal and Sound Therapy, massage therapy, physical therapy, acupuncture, iridology, psychic readings, and more.

I have taken the Harner Foundation's Basic Shamanic workshop and now have Reiki Level 1 & 2, Reiki Master/Teacher and Reiki Drumming Practitioner Certificates, as well as my Holistic Health Practitioner Certificate and Certificates in Spiritual Aromatherapy and Chakra Balancing. It seems I have always been searching for something to fill me up, to complete me. After working with many modalities over time, I finally feel that I like myself. I like the person I have become and I am filled up with love and light again. My spirit is home. I would now like to help others feel this peacefulness, this completeness, and this love.

Several years ago Reiki called to me. My mom's friend Maureen first introduced me to Reiki about twelve years ago. She had her Level 2 Reiki. Maureen was visiting my mom and asked if I wanted a Reiki treatment. I said sure, as I had always been open and willing to try new things. She gave me Reiki while I was sitting in a chair and I felt totally peaceful and relaxed afterward. She asked how I felt and if I had noticed anything. I told her I saw a man, like a monk sitting on a mountaintop. Now when I look back after my further education in Reiki, I am sure it was Mikao Usui that I saw.

After I got married in the year 2000 I focused most of my energy on my marriage, but after my divorce in 2004 I had more time to focus on myself and what I really wanted to do: to be a Reiki Practitioner. I finally had the time to take further training in Reiki and focus on my development as a practitioner.

I love Reiki. It is such a gentle, unobtrusive, healing technique. Since I have always been a rescuer, especially in my intimate relationships (even if they did not want to be helped), I thought Reiki would be a perfect way to help people heal on many levels, emotionally, physically and spiritually. More importantly, they would be coming to me for help, rather than me choosing people to give (sometimes unsolicited) time, energy and help to. I do Reiki self-healing daily as well as Reiki sessions for friends and family. There is a marked difference in my spiritual, mental and physical health and I have had very positive feedback from the Reiki sessions to others. My hope for the future is to open a healing/art studio to help share this beautiful gift of Reiki.

TALES OF A HEALING FAIR: A LITTLE REIKI GOES A LONG WAY!

by Jennifer Lundin Ritchie

I HAVE BEEN PRACTICING REIKI steadily since 1998 in the Greater Vancouver area. In the beginning, I learned Reiki as a means to support myself on my personal journey from depression to wellness. After much personal work, I began to offer Reiki to others, as a Practitioner and finally as a Teacher as well.

Throughout my practice, I have seen some extraordinarily powerful transformations in people as a result of incorporating Reiki treatments into their lives. I have certainly had many unforgettable experiences in private sessions and in the classes I teach, however, some of my most memorable moments have come from short sessions done at healing fairs.

The term "healing fair" can encompass wellness shows, psychic fairs, and health fairs, as well as fundraisers, themed celebrations, and open houses at wellness centres and colleges. Over the years I have worked at all kinds of healing fairs, including big annual events, smaller private events, and many open houses. Sometimes I work alone, sometimes with a small group of practitioner friends, and sometimes with large groups like the Canadian Reiki Association. Each show has a different energy, but all have a few commonalities: they are public, they are busy, and the sessions are short.

The experience of getting a session at a healing fair is not the same as getting a private session. For one, you are often in the middle of a large venue, with crowds bustling around you and loudspeakers announcing the latest demonstration. In addition, while in a private session a person will often book a half hour or an hour session, at a healing fair, Reiki is usually done in 10 or 15 minute sessions. In that short amount of time, a practitioner can usually only do what we call a "mental clearing" (working on the head/brain to de-stress and relax), and perhaps a few spot treatments. However, a lot can be accomplished in that short time and in those conditions!

Some people do not expect that Reiki can work so quickly and so powerfully, and doubt that a public setting could allow for a deep healing. Many people will go to a Reiki booth just to try it out, or to work on some small nagging problem they are experiencing. At a healing fair, I see a lot of headaches, sore feet and backs! While Reiki is definitely suited to these types of everyday aches and pains, and while people are always pleased (and usually surprised) that their short session can remove their immediate pain, the magic of Reiki goes a lot deeper, and can often reveal surprising insights and unforeseen results. Allow me to share some of my healing fair experiences.

One of my earliest shows was at a local herbal dispensary. Their open house had private session rooms for practitioners, which allowed for greater privacy than most fairs. I did a great session on a lady who claimed she was suffering from anxiety due to her work. During her session, I "saw" (with my "third" eye) two young children standing next to the table. I wasn't sure who these children were, but suspected that they were neither "spirit guides" nor her "real" children. I described them to her, and said I thought she might be suffering from separation anxiety. After a moment of shock, she started crying, and told me that I had just described the two main characters in the novel she was writing – the novel she was having trouble finishing because she had become so attached to the characters after spending so much time immersed in the story. She realized that she needed to come to terms with ending her "relationship" to these two children in order to resolve the anxiety related to finishing her book – and finish her book!

Although those children turned out to be fictional, I often delight in the real children who attend healing fairs. They can always "see" the energy at a Reiki booth, and end up transfixed. At one particular show, I saw numerous boisterous children stop short as they turned the corner and saw our booth. All play would cease as they could not tear their eyes away from what we were doing. Some would point, or nudge their playmates. Some nearly gave themselves whiplash trying to ogle us as their parents obliviously pushed their strollers past.

The most memorable healing fair session I did involving a child was at a large local wellness show. A young lady came to my booth complaining of nausea and headaches. She hoped Reiki could help. As I worked I could sense a lot of "debris" throughout her abdomen area. It looked dirty and polluted; as if someone had dumped refuse into a clean pond and it had permeated the water shore to shore. I worked on that area for most of the session, letting the Reiki gently clear away everything that was impeding proper energy flow. At the end of the session she remarked she felt much better, and left.

About half an hour later, she returned with her friend to tell me how amazed she was that her headache and nausea had completely disappeared after our session. She had been feeling almost debilitating nausea and pain every day for the past two months – ever since she had gotten pregnant. Her friend was doubly amazed. I believe the debris and blocks I found in her abdomen were causing complications with her pregnancy. After all, how can a healthy baby grow in a field of debris? Whether this debris was physical or emotional, all "hers" or "picked up" from others, I can not say for sure. I would suspect a mixture of all of the above. But once Reiki cleared the debris and restored her energy flow with pure life force, the pregnancy could continue unimpeded.

Occasionally, I get very concerned for a client when I sense a serious health problem. In the case of a healing fair, you may have just met the client minutes earlier, and may know nothing at all about their history. It can be tricky to know how to proceed. While working at a local health show, a man came to my booth who claimed he just wanted to try Reiki out and see what it was. He did not complain of any health issues or mention any specific goals he wanted to work on. He looked like an average fellow, with nothing overtly wrong. As I worked on his thymus I became very concerned. His immune system was dangerously low. I struggled to determine how I might mention this to him without sounding alarmist or frightening him. Finally, at the end of the session he asked me what I had sensed. I told him I was a little concerned that his immune system was low, and that perhaps he should go for a check up with his doctor just to make sure everything was ok. He alleviated my fears when he laughed: "I'm on chemotherapy!"

Reiki is not just for physical and emotional problems. It can be used to set goals, as one local publisher did on my table at the Vancouver Wellness Show, one of Vancouver's largest annual wellness shows. She wanted to clarify her path, to know which fork in the road to take, and by the end of our session, she had a very clear message of what she needed to do. She was surprised that after months of agonizing over this decision, one short Reiki session at a healing fair could bring everything so sharply into focus and mark so plainly which choice was best for her.

I leave the best for last. Sometimes the healing does not occur only in the client... sometimes the practitioner gets a good dose as well. The most rewarding fair I have worked at to date was the British Columbia Elder's Gathering. It was a gathering of over 3000 Native American Elders, their family, friends, and supporters. The room I was in with the Canadian Reiki Association also held massage therapists and sound healers.

The energy in the place was amazing. Sage smudge wafted

through the space on a continual basis, and our quiet soothing CD music was often drowned out by the amazing traditional native drumming and singing coming from the sound healer's booth. Let me tell you, it really made me want to pick up my drum and pursue a "Reiki Drumming" course!

Every Elder who sat in my chair had an amazing energetic field, whether it was soft and gentle, warm and laughing, proud and strong, or deep and rich. While some of the Elders appeared to have frail bodies, all had strong spirits. There was such an openness and genuineness that issued forth from them. Whether that inner strength and confidence simply comes with age and experience or is a legacy of the powerful First Nations traditions, I could not say. The First Nations have long emphasized the idea of connecting "above and below" in their ceremonies, and receiving wisdom and energy from the Creator or Source, as we do in Reiki. It was such an honour for me to be able to connect with these beautiful wellsprings of wisdom and energy. I worked in awe and in service, and left inspired and enriched.

I am constantly in gratitude to those who climb onto my table, willingly exposing their wounds, their dreams, their lives, in hopes of creating a better existence for themselves. It takes real courage to say "This cannot continue", "I'm ready to let go", "This is what I want", and especially "I need help". I honour each and every one of them in their willingness to step onto and travel that road to happiness, wellness, and wholeness. Some people I see again and again over weeks, months, and years, as they come to private sessions, or proceed through their Reiki classes, but some, like those who grace my stories above, I may only see once in a lifetime. And yet, their stories stay with me and continue to enrich me year after year, and now I hope, they will stay with you as well.

HOW REIKI FOUND ME
by Barb Weston

MANY CLIENTS AND STUDENTS have asked me how I found Reiki and in all honesty, I did not find Reiki, Reiki found me.

As far back into my childhood as I can remember, I have been fascinated with Angels and the role they play in assisting us with our lives. As a child, I was very sensitive to people's feelings and moods and strongly felt their energy. I was a natural mediator and always found myself siding with the "underdog". I strongly disliked seeing other children picked on and would run to their aid and try and comfort them. My heart ached for them and I just could not understand why one human being would treat another in such a cruel way.

Seeing cruelty in the surrounding world caused me to pull inwards and I was very much a "loner" as a child. I found it very difficult to mix with other children as I just did not think the same way they did. I felt like a round peg trying to fit into a square hole and it was easier to just pull away from the other children and be alone with my Angels.

This feeling of not fitting in stayed with me all through my teenage years, into my adulthood and led me gently to my "path". As a teenager, I began reading books such as Jonathon Livingston Seagull and Illusions: The Adventures of a Reluctant Messiah by Richard Bach, The Prophet by Kahlil Gibran, As A Man Thinketh by James Allan, The Precious Present by Spencer Johnson M.D. and The Power Of Your Subconscious Mind by Dr. Joseph Murphy D.R.S., Ph.D., D.D., LL.D. to name a few.

I savoured every word I read and I began to understand that I did not need to fit in with the rest of the world. I was a unique child of God and I was perfectly OK as I was. I realized I was on a wonderful journey of enlightenment with many lessons yet to learn and I was happy to press on, one day at a time. Years went by and more and more I felt as if there was something 'specific" I was supposed to be doing with my life. I did not know exactly what but I felt it would involve helping people on a one to one basis.

On New Year's day of 2000, I awoke and decided I was going to begin my search for "whatever" it was that I was going to do for the rest of my life. I said a prayer to my Guides and Angels asking them to help me find this service or role I was going to play and I begged them not to let me walk past the opportunity when it was ready to present itself to me.

A few days later my husband and I went to an annual psychic fair in Vancouver. I had three Tarot Card readings done by three different readers and each one told me the same thing. They said there was going to be a huge change in what I did to earn my living and that I did not know what it was yet. They would then point skyward and say, "They know you can do it and they have been waiting", and, "it is time for you to awaken."

After hearing that same message three times, I was more puzzled than ever. We walked past another booth and I felt a cold breeze hit the side of my face and it felt as if every hair on my head stood on end. I stopped and looked at the man behind the booth to see if he had a fan blowing to cause this breeze but he did not. He was busy with a client so we kept on walking. A short time later we walked past his booth again and the same thing happened. I felt the cool breeze on my cheek and again it felt as if every hair on my head stood on end. This was no coincidence I thought to myself, as I had asked my Guides and Angels to not let me walk past my opportunity so I took a business card from this booth and two weeks later, I called the man on the card.

His name was David Pilz and he is a Psychic Medium based in Chilliwack. I made an appointment to see David hoping he would be able to give me some insight into what it was I was searching for. Maybe he held the key to this puzzle. I was very comfortable with David and he did several different types of readings for me and told me much the same as the Tarot readers did. I was no further ahead. Then just as I was about to leave, David said, "your aura looks good but your energy is very low. Why don't we do a healing before you go?" I did not come for a healing I was thinking to myself but why not? It was a long drive from North Vancouver to Chilliwack so why not let him do this "healing thing". It certainly would not do any harm.

So up on his healing table I climbed, not having any idea what to expect, but feeling quite calm and relaxed at the same time. He did not explain what he was going to do other than to tell me to hold out my hands as he placed some crystals in them. A few moments later the magic began as he placed his hands over my face and suddenly I felt heat rushing from his palms. With every hand placement I felt heat and a sense of something almost electrical happening in my body. It felt wonderful and magical. An hour rushed by like it was ten minutes and I was told the "healing" was over and I could get up. That was easier said than done, as my body felt like it weighed three hundred pounds. It was dead weight and I needed another ten minutes just to get my arms up off the table let alone my entire body.

The drive home was a blur and as soon as I got in the door I phoned David and made an appointment for another "healing" the very next week. The second "healing" was just as magical as the first one so again, when I arrived back home I called David to make another appointment but this time I was going to ask him if he could teach me how to do this "healing" because suddenly it hit me....this was "it"! This was what I wanted to learn and share with other people. This was what I had been searching for. It was so clear to me.

When I arrived at David's the next week, he congratulated me as I stepped through his door. I became his student that day and that was the day I learned that the "healing" I had received was called Reiki and that David was a Usui Reiki Master as well as a Psychic Medium. My Guides and Angels directed me to David and that was the beginning of my new journey. So you see, I did not find Reiki, as I did not know it even existed. Reiki found me. My life took on a new meaning and a new direction and I feel so very blessed and honoured to be sharing this beautiful gift of Reiki.

CONNECTING WITH CHILDREN
By Nicole LaFleche

A FEW YEARS AGO I had the good fortune to live in Tianjin, China for several months. At that time, Tianjin's population was ten million people including approximately twenty thousand "white skinned" foreigners, so needless to say, being a blond, Caucasian woman, I really stood out in a crowd.

One day I was standing in line at the checkout counter of my local supermarket when I noticed a 3-4 year old little boy staring at me wide eyed and fearful. I smiled at him and he started to cry so loudly that he caught the attention of everyone around as he hid behind his mother's legs. Intuitively, I knew that this little boy had never seen anyone like me before, and I am sure that to him, I looked like some freaky creature from another world.

Not wanting him to become traumatized for life by this experience I almost immediately started sending Reiki love and light to him with my eyes. As I continued to send Reiki, he suddenly poked his little head out and made eye contact with me for a split second. I continued to send Reiki and again he poked his head out and this time looked at me for a while longer. This went on for a few minutes, and each time he would look at me longer and longer, and he even started to smile.

A few minutes into this exchange, his mom said it was time to go. By now, my little friend was gazing at me openly, smiling and laughing, and no longer retreating behind the safety of his mother's legs. When she again prompted him to leave, he stayed rooted in his spot, not breaking eye contact with me. His mom quite literally had to pull him away. As he went with her he kept looking back at me laughing and I laughing back and waving goodbye.

Sending Reiki to this little boy undoubtedly helped him to release the fear he was experiencing when he first saw me, and possible life time trauma. I am so grateful that I was able to send Reiki to him right away. It made me realize how open and readily accepting children are to this beautiful, peaceful energy. This experience prompted me to teach Reiki to children and because of this, I have many more beautiful memories filed away and I value and cherish them all!

REIKI WORKS!
By Francesca Molinari

MY FIRST ATTUNEMENT TO REIKI happened in 1999. I remember being fairly sceptical considering even more sceptical people surrounded me for the most part. My mom was the one who dragged me to the attunement because she wanted to learn more about Reiki. I just went along for the ride, after all you never know. Here I am, a few years later going for my Reiki Master certification as one of my life commitments.

I am originally from Italy, my family and I moved to Canada in 1997 and so far it has been an interesting journey. I was twenty-four at the time of our family's move. I recently decided to break away from my family business and start my own Reiki practice. Since I decided to do this things have been slowly happening to make my goal become closer and closer. I have learned and keep learning so much but the biggest lesson has been the one of gratitude. For a person who was so negative, always asking why the heck she decided to come back into this "crappy" world I became the person who would accept the things I cannot change and do my best to better what I could.

Reiki would always come to me in my darkest moments when I could not stop crying from the desperation I felt inside, when everything seemed lost. An example of what I mean occurred when I decided to have an abortion because the partner I was with during that time turned out to be an unsuitable parent and I felt I could not put a baby in such a situation. That experience devastated my body first, then my soul. Guilt started to set in, depression, and constant suicidal thoughts. The doctor put me on light anti-depressants and he said to me that they were really light but my body, already devastated from the recent incident, simply did not like them and I was left with feeling dull and fuzzy for most of the day, and not hungry at all. I stopped eating food for the most part because even looking at it would make me feel sick, so I went off the anti-depressants and I started self-medicating instead with herbs and Reiki. Reiki was always there with me and I used it many times during this difficult period. My dog, that also went through similar stress as I did during this time enjoyed the change and was grateful to receive Reiki too. She is still here with me and happy to continue receiving Reiki every night.

When Reiki would come to me, especially during really stressful moments, it would feel like a warm, fuzzy feeling at first in my solar plexus area, then expanded to the rest of the body, bringing a deep feeling of relaxation and peace. Over time, it helped me give up smoking and most of those depressing and negative reoccurring thoughts and feelings I used to have. Reiki was never there to change my reality. It was there to help me heal and understand that while I cannot change certain things, I could decide to be happy, as much as possible, and not let other events and people negatively affect me. I will never forget my abortion and what I went through but now I look at it differently.

The other important event that happened was with my father who almost died of heart failure, after having a heart attack without realizing it. My Dad is in fact the best example of a person who did not really believe in Reiki and then "converted" his thinking because of the very real experience he had about nine months ago.

When my mom and I took my Dad into the emergency room, we had no idea what we were in for. He had just been diagnosed with colon cancer and was scheduled that week for an operation to remove it. Luckily, he had a heart attack the previous weekend otherwise he would have probably died under the knife because his heart would have failed! So, from a tragedy a really good thing turned out, he was saved!

The doctors were working hard, trying to figure out what was wrong with his heart when we arrived at the hospital emergency room. At first, they did not even know it was the heart and then after we told them my Dad had a history of heart problems and family members who had died of heart attacks, they started to look into it more closely. It took them about twenty-four hours to figure out his problem and fix it. Thank God they are good at their work and they saved him but the worst was not over. He now had to come out of the induced coma and start recovering.

The heart was badly damaged, so badly that the doctors themselves told us they still could not figure out how he could have been alive. Ironically, I had given my Dad Reiki about four months prior and I had felt the issues in the heart, his liver and intestine, exactly where he had the cancer. I think part of me did not want to believe my Dad could have heart issues as well, knowing his family history! I felt I could not tell the doctors that I knew Reiki because I worried most of them would think it was all fantasy.

After five long days my Dad woke up and I was there at the foot of his bed and he told me then that he saw a purple light in the corner of his room after asking for help. He knew he needed help in order to heal and all of a sudden he said he was full of Reiki.

Well, to this day I think he survived because he asked for Reiki help combined with the prompt procedure the doctors performed on him. I am convinced this combination is what helped my Dad survive from the incredible amount of damage to his heart, much to the disbelief of his doctors. His survival and story proved it to me how powerful and amazing energy healing can be. Reiki to me is like blood, we all should have it and enjoy its benefits.

While my Dad is not out of the woods yet, it is his choice to practice Reiki and meditation, he is doing a lot better. A part of his heart died about five years prior when he had his first heart attack that was mistaken for an ulcer in the duodenum. His heart has been working at about 40% for the past nine months but he is improving every day.

My Dad is also the proof that you do not have to believe in Reiki for it to work but you do have to want to heal. Reiki can never be imposed on others and that is another wonderful quality of this healing energy that interested me so much when I first started using it. I believe we are all responsible for our own health and I consider the doctors as guidance to take the right decisions and Reiki is part of my daily choices.

In the past year, I have focused on building my Reiki practice and while challenging; it has been a lot of fun. When you get enough people telling you how you have a gift and how they want to refer people to you, I take it as a sign that I am going in the right direction. I love the fact that I could never harm anybody with it through human error. I came from stress and problems and now with the help of Reiki, all I see is peace and joy. Reiki works, try it for yourself. It is easy to learn, very affordable and it works well with any other healing modality, medicines or situation.

ANGEL WINGS
by Sherri Daun

I WAS CONDUCTING A REIKI treatment with a client in my office one summer day in 2006. My client was snoozing gently on the massage table and I was relaxed as the result of so much Reiki energy traveling through my body and hands. During treatments, I will occasionally become aware of the spiritual presence of Mikao Usui; the deceased founder of Reiki. I can with my mind's eye and my mind's ear, see and hear his astral body and speech. Sometimes Mr. Usui will instruct me as to where to place my hands or he would challenge my subtle senses, asking, "You feel disturbance here, but where is the source of the problem?"

Thus, I was not surprised when I became aware of Mr. Usui and three young Japanese men in the room with me that summer's day. The young Japanese men stood across from me and placed their hands on top of my client's torso. Mr. Usui stood to my right. My hands were resting on my client's stomach and I began to feel the Reiki that was emanating from the astral men's hands fill my client's body.

My client stirred, looked at my hands, and remarked, "My right side just got very hot. It feels like your hands are on this side but they are on the other side."

"Reiki can travel anywhere it pleases in your body. Your body will draw what it wants, where it wants. Even though my hands may be on this side, you may feel the Reiki on the other side, or even in your toes!" I informed him truthfully, but I did not disclose the presence of the astral helpers for I did not want to scare my client.

"I would have sworn your hands were on my other side if I

didn't open my eyes and see for myself," my client murmured as he returned to his light slumber.

I watched Mr. Usui scan my client's body with his eyes and then nod his head in understanding. He had finished his diagnosis. Mr. Usui turned his gaze to me and asked, "What do you detect?"

I gave him my reply with my thoughts.

"What do you think is going on in those areas?"

This was a difficult question to answer for I only get feeble impressions when I feel byosen, (energy imbalances or energy depletion), in clients. With silent thoughts, I relayed all that I could detect in the client's body to my astral teacher.

Mr. Usui pointed to the largest byosen and asked, "This is where it sits, but where is its source? Where in the body does this disturbance come from?"

I scanned my client's head and torso with my eyes, hoping to see a shift, a spark of light, a pull, a tingling, anything that would give me a clue as to where the source of the byosen was situated, but I sensed nothing.

I released a sigh and complained in my thoughts, "Usui! I look and I look but I never find. It's so hard for me. All I know is that these areas have very bad byosen and I have to treat here. I do not know how you can find the source of disease so fast. You are so good at this, but I'm not that good yet."

Mr. Usui ignored my grumbling and glanced at his astral companions. The Japanese men nodded in understanding then moved their hands to treat new areas of my client's body. I saw great shifts in my client's energetic system and I wondered how this affected my client.

My client's face contorted. The brow furrowed and the lips pursed then stretched to form awkward smiles and frowns. My client did not wake up and I was glad for that. I could not explain what was happening.

Suddenly, from my client's torso, two great white lights erupted and sprayed light into the room. I looked questioningly to Mr. Usui, but he only nodded his head. I was confused for a moment until it occurred to me that Mr. Usui was showing me the byosen's source. This was where he wanted me to place my hands.

I moved into position. I felt powerful Reiki pass through my body and I was a bit overwhelmed by it. I felt Reiki pour out of my eyes and, as I looked across the room, any object I saw was quickly filled with Reiki. I felt a thick energy erupt from my back at two points near my shoulder blades. I felt as if my bio-essence, an internal thick and brilliant white life energy, exploded from my back and filled the space behind me.

This was a brand new experience for me and, although I was not afraid, I was extremely curious as to what was going on. I looked to Mr. Usui for an explanation and he told me to look up. I quickly checked to see if my client was still asleep. I did not want to look like a fool if my client saw me gawk at the ceiling!

My client seemed to be asleep. I took a chance and looked up. A vortex formed in the ceiling. Far into the vortex, about two stories high, a brilliant point of light appeared. I knew what this was! I had seen this once before.

Several years earlier, when I was given the Reiki ability, I became aware of a brilliant white star or light point situated about two stories above my head. A long, thin, white spire erupted from the crown of my head and probed upwards until it touched the point above.

A voice next to my ear said, "That is your contact, your connection to the Reiki energy source."

Recognizing this point of light, I asked Mr. Usui, "Why are you showing me my Reiki connection?"

His words were garbled to my ear, "It is scherws smeeww whoo."

I asked him to speak again and I focused my mind to comprehend the astral speech, "You are ddreeoo shue dree"

I sighed. This has happened before. If I am presented new ideas and concepts or shown new visuals that I have never known or seen before, often I am unable to comprehend or clearly see what the spirit world is trying to communicate with me. I was greatly saddened that I could not discern the nature of the events.

I had only a moment to ponder my bad fortune for I was quickly distracted. The thick, white, bio-essence energy expanded and took an astounding form!

Two great, brilliant, white feathered, wings took shape and spread outwards into the room. The wings were thick and long, consisting of many large feathers. Each wing was about three meters long and the feathers themselves were quite wide, perhaps forty-five centimetres long. They looked just like the wings one sees in depictions of Angels. My Angel wings stretched and fluttered for a moment and then rested overtop my client and the Japanese men in a protective stance.

Whoa! Why do I have wings? I thought to myself in amazement.

The Japanese men broke into laughter.

"She thinks they are wings!" I heard the men say to each other, "She doesn't know what it is!"

Many questions were forming in my mind, but Mr. Usui spoke before I could inquire.

He said with a deep sigh, "Sherri, the wings are the result of a deeper connection to the Reiki source."

I could sense Mr. Usui's emotions. There was so much he wanted to explain but my mind could not perceive his astral words. I knew his explanation was incomplete.

My Angel wings remained with me until the end of the treatment. Soon enough, the wings lost their form and returned to the bright, white, bio-essence. The essence then merged into my body at the two points from which they erupted. Mr. Usui and the Japanese men left my awareness and my client roused from a sleepy state. I asked my client questions about the treatment, secretly hoping to discover if anything out of the ordinary was experienced, but my client did not disclose anything remarkable.

Months passed and I began to doubt my experience. I wondered, *were the Angel wings truly real or had I daydreamed them?* I received an unexpected answer when a Reiki Master Student and I were philosophizing about the subject of Reiki.

My student commented, "You know Sherri, I should probably not tell you this, but did you know, great white wings came out of my back and covered my client and me? It was beautiful! They looked just like Angel wings. They had big, bright white feathers and the wings were large and full."

Needless to say, I was extremely excited to hear that I was not alone in my astounding and mysterious experience. I asked my student what meaning or purpose she felt existed in the incident.

She wisely replied, "It's love. The wings are an expression of great love."

I could not have thought of a better explanation than that.

HUMMINGBIRD ANGELS
by Mary Charette

ONE EVENING during my last piano lesson, I received a call from my father-in-law. He was completely distressed at finding a tiny bird on his porch and did not know what to do with it. I told him to get a warm hot water bottle, wrap it in a towel and place it and the little bird in a shoebox and bring the little bird to me.

I quickly sprung into action and got a hold of a birdcage so I would have something to keep the little bird in overnight. When the bird arrived, I peeked into the shoebox and discovered it was a little humming bird. It looked up at me but did not move as it was in shock.

I kept the bird in the shoebox with the hot water bottle but placed the box into the bird cage and covered the cage with a towel so the space was dark. I placed my hands on either side of the cage and started beaming Reiki to the little bird. I peeked in every so often and the little bird looked me in the eyes as if to say, "Please keep going and please stop peeking". I did this for an hour.

The next morning I was very nervous to lift the towel. I peeked first and could see the little bird was sitting in the towel nest we had placed in the cage. When I lifted the towel the little bird started fluttering like crazy. I put the towel back over the cage and decided to release the bird closer to where it had "crashed". It was completely revived and flew off like a little dart.

But this is not where the story ends and continues about two weeks later; I was going through a serious crisis. I had gone for a Reiki treatment which was extremely intense where I was working to release a lot of very negative ties from a past relationship. I got home from the treatment quite exhausted and decided to go and sit in my garden and meditate under my apple tree. I was not there for more than ten minutes and I was completely surrounded by hummingbirds. They were fluttering around my head and zooming up to my face, looking me in the eyes and zooming off. I felt like little healing angels surrounded me.

They stayed for about five minutes and then fluttered into the bushes and trees around my garden. It was one of the most magical moments of my life. It was as if they were saying, "You helped one of us, and now we are helping you". Any negative feelings that were still lingering inside of me were completely taken away.

Every time I see humming birds in my garden, they lift my spirits and remind me to smile. They are my little garden angels.

PIGMY OWL
by Linda Buhler

A COUPLE OF YEARS AGO, the owl rehab center in my town called me to come in and do some Reiki for a small pigmy owl in their center. I agreed to help and went into the center to meet the small owl. The little owl was in a flight pen which was a large room with cement walls and one little window that looked outside to let in light. A second window was also quite small and allowed viewers to look in from inside the building.

Inside the flight room, there was sawdust on the floor, several little stumps and a tree limb that led up to an eye-level shelf for the birds to perch on. A little nest was placed in the corner where the limb met the shelf so the birds could get up higher and feel protected. When I went in to the center, the small male pigmy owl was in the room on the floor in the sawdust. I had no idea how I was going to treat him because I could not actually pick him up or touch him as he his condition was not very good. So I set about for the first time in my life, learning how to communicate with a bird!

I finally sat down on one of the little stumps, cleared my mind and began visualising the owl moving from where he was in the sawdust, jumping onto the shortest stump and then making his way from one stump to another towards the tree limb. Then I visualized him reaching the limb safely and continuing his journey up higher so he could eventually reach the shelf that was near my eye level. From there I could then do Reiki on him.

I tried to use my mind to explain to him what I wanted him to do. Animals think in pictures so you have to visualize things in pictures. I did my best to explain what it was that I wanted him to do. I also told him that I wanted to help him by giving him Reiki. I also acknowledged him, told him I respected him and finally that I felt honoured to be the one asked to come and help him. After spending about ten minutes sending him these visual pictures using my mind, nothing happened. So I left the room, thinking I would give him space to do what I had pictured and sure enough, he did exactly what I wanted him to do! He went from stump to stump, walked sideways up the limb and ended up on the little shelf. When I came in, he was at my eye level, making it much easier for me to beam Reiki energy to him.

He was an amazing little bird. He was very open to doing the Reiki and he had internal injuries that I could "see" when I scanned him. I felt he was very in tune and open to the Reiki. When I did Reiki on him, I felt his heart center did not match a bird of his size. I do not know how to explain what I mean other than to say he had the heart of an eagle. It was huge! It was unbelievable to me how such a small bird could have such a huge heart. This little bird had the heart of a fearless, courageous and brave bird.

I went several days in a row to the owl rehabilitation center and each day I went in, the pigmy owl was on the floor in the sawdust. So each day I went in, I sat down and visualized what I needed him to do, acknowledged him and each day he walked up and did what I asked him to do. I was very excited about the fact that I was able to communicate with him. I had another staff member come in to witness the process and explained to her what I was doing, sending the owl the visualization and then coming out of the room to give him space to move. This time the both of us watched him do what I had asked him to do. It validated the whole experience for me and strengthened my belief that I was doing the right thing, communicating with the owl using the visualisations I was sending him.

On the very last day that I went back to the rehabilitation center, I knew the pigmy owl was ready to leave this world. He was still on the shelf when I went in. I started doing Reiki on him for several minutes and felt like maybe it was not going to help. I also did some Tellington Touch on him and it is always done on birds using a feather. I was using an eagle feather to do the Tellington Touch and he was very open to me doing this.

I cupped my hands and he allowed me to beam Reiki to him and when I used the eagle feather, he allowed me to touch him with the tip of the feather and he puffed up a little and even raised his wings up so I could get underneath them. It is almost like doing a very gentle massage with the tip of the feather and because it is feather light, it was acceptable to him.

Finally I felt like it was time for me to leave. I said goodbye to him, told him that I knew he was leaving. I also told him I was honoured to be part of his life and I acknowledged that I knew it was time for him to go. As I started to pull my hands away, he reached out with his little claw and wrapped it around my thumb and held me there doing Reiki until he passed away. It was the most awesome experience that I've had in my life working with animals. There is no doubt in my mind that Reiki helped him make that transition. When he left, it was like an eagle soared.

GILDA THE GOLDFISH
By Mary Charette

GILDA CAME INTO MY LIFE without any forethought. I was strolling through a pet store in the mall and spotted this ridiculously happy little fish in a tank with 3 dead fish. I thought "I have to get this little angel out of there". I purchased the full aquarium set and $200 later, Gilda was enjoying her luxurious habitat in our kitchen. Everybody loves Gilda because she is a very interactive goldfish. She comes to the glass to see what is going on. She waits for her food in the same spot every morning and she is extremely playful.

Cleaning out the tank is very stressful for fish. I try to make the process as stress free as possible by putting her into a "waiting" bowl while I clean and vacuum the tank. On one such occasion, to my horror, Gilda was totally belly up in her "waiting bowl" and was not moving. I touched her belly which got her moving but she just kept rolling onto her back. I was so upset. I started sending her Reiki and that seemed to temporarily revive her while I finished getting her tank ready. Once I put her back in the tank she continued to roll onto her back so I decided that she needed a full Reiki treatment. After the first fifteen minutes she was swimming from hand to hand on the sides of the tank. By the end she was zipping around as usual. Reiki had completely revived her and she was feeling fantastic.

I try to make time for Gilda every week. She only needs about fifteen minutes of Reiki but she really enjoys it. She swims happily from hand to hand, wiggling her beautiful tail and swishing her fins.

WORKING WITH ANIMALS...
REIKI'S LITTLE MIRACLES
by Sue Bagust

PART ONE

If you would like to learn humility, work with animals. Animals are honest and will politely let you know exactly what they want and need. Most animals seem to really enjoy receiving Reiki. One of our cats would even jump up onto the Reiki table to try to join in any Reiki session by offering "paws on" while we did "hands on".

I have been told by another Reiki practitioner that horses would even turn to nudge his hands into the correct position, before relaxing into the Reiki he was offering. I have sent Reiki to many beings since I was first introduced to Reiki in 1991 and have thoroughly enjoyed seeing Reiki work and have witnessed first-hand the difference that Reiki can make in any situation. Some of my most memorable Reiki experiences have been working with animals.

One of the most unforgettable animals I have worked with was a spoiled white cat that had damaged his throat and could not swallow past the scar tissue. His veterinarian suggested that if the cat did not prosper on a diet of pureed cat food then the kindest act may be euthanasia rather than slow starvation. The cat's owner was distraught so we tried Reiki and truthfully I think the cat's owner would have tried anything by that stage as she was very upset.

The cat ignored me for at least half an hour, finally decided to sniff my hands, then rolled over and totally accepted the Reiki offered, but only for five minutes. I had to go back the next night to offer more Reiki, which the pampered puss accepted, but again only for five minutes. I worked in five-minute sessions over a number of nights. It seemed the cat knew what it needed because he not only thrived on the pureed cat food, but in time, the scar tissue eventually softened and decreased so he could eat normal food again.

Another interesting cat experience was with a very determined black cat named Prushka. She was an experienced "escapologist" (escape artist) and always managed to get out of her owner's house whenever she wished. She also enjoyed "sharing" when Reiki was being practised, but once she was pregnant with her first litter she became a Reiki thief. I would be quietly watching TV, when suddenly I would realise that I was channelling Reiki. Sure enough, Prushka had escaped again from her owners and somehow managed to get herself into my home, on my couch, under my hand. As soon as she realised that I was aware of her presence she would start to purr loudly, but until that point would she just lay quietly, gracefully accepting Reiki. Prushka visited me nearly every night while she was pregnant, until she produced six healthy, large kittens with a minimum of fuss, after which she stopped visiting and happily stayed home with her family.

PART TWO

The slowest animals to accept Reiki in my experience have been birds. A Peaceful Dove had knocked itself senseless trying to fly through a window. When I found it, it was limp and ants had moved in. I brushed the ants off and sat for forty minutes offering Reiki until I felt the bird begin to stir. By this time, another Peaceful Dove had flown to a nearby tree and chattered as she watched. I did wonder if she was giving me instructions. The second bird stayed until the first bird revived enough to hold onto a branch by itself (about ten to fifteen minutes later) and then they flew off together about five minutes after that. The observer bird did not stop talking, even when they flew away. The Reiki bird was flying a bit erratically at first, so perhaps the observer bird was still issuing instructions by doing the bird equivalent of back seat driving (or flying).

Another example of practicing Reiki on birds occurred when I worked with a Superb Fruit Dove. This dove had been caught by a cat, did not appear to be injured, but certainly did not want to fly. Initially I gave Reiki for around an hour, then we put the dove into a box to stay quiet overnight. The next morning, after another Reiki session for the dove, both my husband and I tried to get the dove to fly. The dove was equally determined to stay in our hands so we gave up, gave it a cage, food and more Reiki. We tried again the next morning but the dove just would not fly. After three days of Reiki twice a day and food, I had to make a road trip to another town for a Reiki weekend. The dove eventually flew but only after it realized that it was not going to get any more Reiki on demand!

Reiki truly is full of little miracles as my first Reiki teacher told me back in 1991. I feel blessed that I have experienced so many of these little miracles in the years since I have been practising Reiki. Although it is great to offer Reiki to humans because you can feel and see Reiki working (for example, healthy skin colour coming back to a face during a treatment and a brighter more focused look) I still enjoy working with animals. Animals just test the feeling, and if they like it take what is offered, they use it and get on with life. Now that is my definition of a good Reiki treatment!

RIBO

By Tania Bakas

ONE MORNING MY DOG, Ribo was sitting on the bed staring at me. She had a sad "look" on her face and from where I was sitting she looked quite strange. I went a little closer to see her and what I saw was very scary. There was a very large lump protruding from the side of her eye socket. It was red and looked very irritated. I was terrified. I called the veterinarian immediately and got their answering machine. So I left a message and proceeded to panic. I did not know what to do for my little angel.

Then I thought to myself, "I will just do some Reiki on her and see if she feels a little better." Usually Ribo will not sit long for a Reiki session so I decided to "beam" the Reiki energy from about a foot's distance. She closed her eyes and allowed the energy to flow. Five minutes later I placed my hands under her jaw and flowed some more Reiki. She sat there for about 5 more minutes before wanting to move around again. So I gave her a little break and went on to do some housework while I waited for the veterinarian to call back.

About an hour went by and I went to check on her. I still had that visual of the lump on her eye and I just wanted to cry because I felt so terrible for her. She was sleeping on the bed and she heard me enter the room. She lifted her head, looked at me and I looked at her eyes and saw the lump had disappeared! That huge ugly "thing" had vanished!

She gradually became more playful throughout the day and it was as if nothing had ever happened to her. Every day with Reiki is an experience of miracles, little and big. I am so grateful that this loving energy has entered my world as it has made my life so much more fulfilling and joyous.

BELLA
By Linda Buhler

A FRIEND OF MINE had a little Boston Bull Terrier named Bella. This little dog was two years old and full of energy like they are supposed to be at that age. She would run around everywhere and was always a happy-go-lucky dog. My friend had to take two months and go to Squamish where a lot of stressful things had happened. Her son was in an accident so Bella was left with some of her friends while she was caring for her son. Bella was left alone more than she was accustomed to, sometimes at home and sometimes in the car.

We were not sure if it was a tick bite, a spider bite or the trauma of being left with her friends but when the owner picked up Bella after two months, she was appalled at the state of health the dog was in. It was as if Bella had been replaced by a totally different dog!

My friend called me from the car on her drive home and stopped at my house once she arrived back in town. She set the dog down in my kitchen and Bella was hardly able to hold herself up and had lost about ¾ of her weight. Bella's knee was in bad shape and the entire rear leg was hanging, unable to be used.

Right away we made an appointment with a holistic vet and we went as soon as they could get us in. By the time we got up there, the dog could no longer turn over. We had to hold Bella up to do her business, to eat, to drink and she could not stand up on her own. When we arrived at the veterinary clinic, there was some debate over performing surgery to fix Bella's leg because the veterinarian was not sure she was strong enough to survive the surgery. One of the options discussed was to put Bella down. The doctor said that she wanted to give Bella one more week because she deserved a second chance so we brought her back home. I went 2-3 times a day to Bella's house to give her Reiki, Tellington Touch and to clear her aura.

Each day she became a little stronger and started greeting me at the door, sometimes running, and would lay down right there for me to do Reiki. She also improved enough to flip herself over for me to do Reiki on her other side. Most days she would ask for Reiki by waiting at the door for me to arrive and give her Reiki. My girlfriend would call and say that Bella was not feeling well and was waiting at the door for me to arrive. I went every day for two months and did Reiki on this little dog. She only became stronger and stronger over time. She had gained weight, was running around the orchard, although she still had the leg problem, she was a normal happy girl again. I know it was because she had all of the negative energy cleared and had her energy balanced a couple of times a day that it helped her become strong again.

When the time came she no longer needed the Reiki I had been giving her, she would no longer lay still or flip over automatically. Instead, she would lick my hand or try to get me to play ball with her to distract me. That dog is a true Reiki story. To this day, when she is not feeling well, my friend calls me and tells me that Bella is waiting for me by the door. She will lay down by the same stool that I sit on to give her Reiki and waits for me. She is totally aware of what it is doing for her and she is an awesome little girl.

BASIL
by Pat Sweet

I OCCASIONALLY go to a local cat foster home and do Reiki for the cats there. Sometimes they are not interested and wander off but most seem to like it. They can obviously see/feel the Reiki because sometimes I get a small crowd and they sniff round my fingers and the backs of my hands.

Basil was a youngish cat there, gentle and quiet with a soft cinnamon coloured coat and pale copper eyes. Basil had large bald patches on his flanks. His fosterer had tried everything including a visit to the local and excellent veterinary practice that could not find anything wrong. The fosterer also tried homeopathic treatment but his condition continued to worsen. I spoke to Basil and asked if he would like some Reiki and he gave a little chirrup and gazed trustingly at me. What a little heartbreaker!

I "scanned" him and it felt "cold" over the patches. I picked him up and cuddled him because that seemed the easiest way to get the Reiki directly on the patches. Happily, he enjoyed the experience and I could feel the Reiki flowing in very strongly. After I while I put him back on the dresser. He mewed at me and stretched a front paw up to me so of course I wanted to take him home with me that instant – that was the hard bit.

On the next visit (two weeks later), there was a fine growth of fur over most of the bald part. He was sleeping on a shelf too high up for me to reach so I beamed the Reiki to him. I could feel a strong flow as before and although he continued to sleep, he did give a lovely gentle stretch. One month later, I went back and could not see Basil. When I asked his fosterer, she said he had been re-homed to a lovely couple. I hardly dared ask but she said,

"Yes, all his fur had grown back just as if it had never been gone". His fosterer was later invited to tea by Basil's new owners and was able to report Basil was happy and adored and living in the lap of luxury.

A FLYING
FOX WITH ATTITUDE
By Sue Bagust

ONE MEMORABLE REIKI experience was working with a flying fox. He was very angry after being hung up on barbed wire at Lavarack Army Barracks. When he was rescued he was incredibly stressed and acted violently towards any human he could reach. He also was not the least bit interested in eating, which was more of a worry. I offered Reiki to the flying fox (without going too near his cage – I am not that brave), and within minutes he decided that food was worth eating after all, even though he was still ready to rip the hands off any human that came too close! For the initial feeds, the flying fox would settle and accept food from a pipette but only as long as the Reiki flowed along with the food.

After he learned how to accept food from humans, the little flying fox thrived. Wildlife caretakers looked after him and taught him how to find food himself as he grew in strength. When he was big enough he was released back into the wild at a flying fox colony in tropical rainforest near Atherton, North Queensland.

Distance Reiki
& Transition

ASSISTING DURING TRANSITION
by M.F.B

THIS STORY OF INSPIRATION is about a journey with Alzheimer's. The nature of this disease often causes a loss of communication skills. Not being able to even put a sentence together is very distressing, as those afflicted are still very much "present" and wish to communicate. The absolute sense of "not being heard" is quite incredible.

The person I worked with through this experience is my Father. I felt that he would not be the type of person that would be open to any type of hands-on treatment, so I was doing a lot of distance Reiki treatments for him. The duration of his illness was about four years and eventually reached a devastating stage that required him to be in a care facility.

My Father was a great Dad in every sense, there was never a doubt that he loved his children, but he had been quite reserved in showing affection to us when we were younger. What really became obvious when I started doing Reiki for him was that some of these inhibitions, mental-emotional blocks and unproductive habits that he had held onto for many years, started to break down. It became noticeable that he really wanted to reach out and hug. Prior to starting the treatments he would normally hold himself back. With Reiki he started to just "be" and allow himself to receive, to hug and hold hands and that need increased as he became progressively sicker.

Reiki was a wonderful gift for him to receive and to be able to experience. With the lack of communication that sets in with

Alzheimer's at least he was able to release some old habits that would have previously held him back from expressing himself. He even sat back and cried with me a couple of times.

I was traveling quite a bit and would do distance treatments for him every day, sometimes more than once a day. He was as vivid and clear in distance treatments as he was in person because of the spiritual connection that had started to grow for him.

The mental-emotional body would become so active that I could clearly feel that he was reviewing times of his life where he felt a lot of regret. I felt it was all being healed and released, preparing him for his transition to be more spiritually at peace. Even though the Alzheimer's was progressing I saw that he was becoming more relaxed. Understanding Reiki, I saw that he had a peaceful energy about him while often others entering his space would take his calmness at face value assuming that he simply could not interact but I knew there was more to it.

When I would visit my father at the care facility, several of the staff were aware of the Reiki treatments I was providing for him. They all knew my Dad really well and they would know when I had just given him a treatment. Not because they had seen me treating him but because his whole demeanour would change. He had received so much Reiki over time that they were able to keep certain medications on a low dosage.

I was there with Dad when he passed away and was doing Reiki for him during this time. He was in a lot of pain and was heavily medicated. Spiritually it was very noticeable that he was trying to leave his body but the drugs were like an "anchor" – they were so low in vibration and made it difficult for him. He would reach out energetically while I was sitting there with him and ask for more Reiki. It was so perceptible that he was reaching out for help and he had reached an awareness of being ready to "leave". I believe he understood that the Reiki was helping him release "energetic anchors", somehow elevating his "vibration" so that he would be able to leave.

Witnessing a person go through transition may not be the ideal situation for one to want to participate in, considering the grief involved. On the other hand, having been able to witness the spiritual healing that took place in the last four years of my father's life was incredible. I was there to see his accomplishment of being able to release old tension. Although outwardly he appeared to be in a lot of pain, spiritually he was able to experience a smooth and relaxed transition.

THE MAGIC OF REIKI
by Liesel Meuris

AFTER HAVING PRACTICED REIKI for 15 years, I have experienced many instances of Reiki's power. One of the most intriguing occasions for me happened during the process of distant attuning/reiju using a proxy. My first student in Melbourne, since moving here, was of Thai origin and incredibly excited about what happened for her in taking on Reiki. In her first attunement/reiju her guide, Quan Yin appeared to her, fully manifested. Despite the fact that I was attuning/reiju her in a completely different space, I could also feel the intensity of the energy that arrived. Since then she continues to request healings and attunements/reiju from me for her family in Thailand.

Since we have been sending Reiki energy and distant attunements/reiju to my student's family, one of her sisters feels fully connected and is using Reiki to help others with their healing. Another sister who has been unsuccessful with Invitro Fertilization (IVF) has been able to harvest healthy eggs and is awaiting the implants.

When I attuned/reiju her mother, we were unable to reach her beforehand, however my student felt comfortable to go ahead. I used her as the proxy to connect with her mother and at the end of the attunement/reiju she said that she "saw" herself in a temple. When she rang her mother the next day, she found out that her mother was in a temple at the time we sent the attunement/reiju. I continue to be amazed with the "divine power" of Reiki.

DISTANCE
HEALING FOR ANIMALS
by M.F.B

I HAVE WORKED extensively with animals during transition and illness. Distance Reiki has proven beneficial in situations where the physical body is in distress. When the body is suffering, it may be difficult to accept spiritual healing as the focus is on the physical distress present. Distance Reiki can access the energy bodies without involving the physical body.

For me it has been a journey of connecting with animals at their transition time and being able to pass back messages to their owners. Animals cannot speak to their people in order to have them understand what it is they are going through in the last moments or hours of their life. People will frequently ask if the animal "stayed around" and sometimes I have an answer, sometimes I do not. I am not a psychic; I find I am able to pick up different vibrations from the different energy bodies in more of a sentient way. This helps me to clarify for people the issues surrounding their animals and helps them put to rest what they do not understand. I have done treatments for the animals in person prior to their transition and felt that the owners were able to recognize positive changes in their animals just before transitioning.

I have assisted many family pets in their transition and have worked with animals that were very ill and old, often in the process of leaving. Doing Reiki for them prior to transition showed huge psychological changes in many situations where the owners could see that the Reiki treatments were working and so decided to add Reiki to benefit their pet during transition. Sometimes, it is difficult for owners to "wrap their brains around it" [benefits of Reiki] but it has proven to be something really valuable in terms of connecting with spirit and helping to release any of the anchors that are holding the animals here on the Earth plane. Reiki is so gentle with doing this.

TRANSITION
By M.F.B

I HAD A CLIENT who was a medical practitioner. He was diagnosed with cancer. He started using Reiki because he had heard that after you have chemotherapy, Reiki could assist you to recover quicker and minimize the effects of the treatments. I started doing Reiki for him. I could hear in his words and feel how he was trying to not be so "book learned" but to allow himself to just be open and understand from a different place.

He struggled incredibly with allowing this openness and we talked about how a medical practitioner such as himself, could look at a patient and tell them they have six months to live without offering them any hope. He himself had been that person, delivering news like this many times. Now that he had been diagnosed with cancer and someone else had said to him, "You have 'x' amount of time to live", he began to see it from both sides.

We discussed about how there may be truth to the statement but it did not necessarily mean that the diagnosed illness is what one is going to die from. The moment we are born, we are dying and for the western trained physician that my client was, he found that his whole way of thinking started to change. The change began because now he was able to view his diagnosis through his own personal experience, being on the receiving end of all of it. In a conversation we discussed how from the medical perspective, notifying the patient of the time they have left gives them time to finalize their life, and how that is not what most people do; they just live in fear. We are so much more than the physical body and the medical system needs to offer the necessary mental, emotional and spiritual support required.

My client was quite wealthy and tried all kinds of cancer treatments. He went to anyone that claimed they could cure cancer, and every time he would come back defeated because he would place his power in someone else. Each time when he would come back, he would say that the only thing that gave him hope was the thought of receiving Reiki to aid him in gaining strength again.

Whenever he would travel he would plan his sessions with Reiki practitioners in the countries that he visited so that he could keep up with his Reiki treatments. After some time, he asked if instead I could just do distance treatments for him while he travelled. We would always set a time and he would get himself relaxed and would tell me afterwards how he could feel the treatment happening. He could feel when I connected with him, and how all of a sudden he would become clearer, feel more empowered, and in different areas of his body where he may have been holding stress, he felt more relaxed. He knew when the treatment would begin and when it would stop.

I had visited with him a couple of weeks before he passed away. After our visit, he left on another trip. When he passed away, I was doing a distance treatment on someone else and during the session, I kept feeling like I was being intruded upon by him. Spiritually he was reaching out while his body was transitioning. There was such a sense of understanding for him when he was connected with Reiki – how much better he felt, how much more clear and empowered he was. He was reaching out for Reiki during his transition, seeking more clarity and assistance.

A week later I heard of his passing and the friend who informed me knew of the exact time it had happened. I backtracked into my journal and verified that indeed his passing happened during the distance treatment I was doing for another person, confirming my feeling it had been him.

AFTERWORD

WE SINCERELY HOPE that the stories collected here have been enjoyed by you, our readers. It is our hope that we have connected you with some of the benefits of Reiki and perhaps provided a smile, a tear or a little dose of hope and inspiration in your daily life. Our humble desire is that we have inspired you enough to tell a friend or family member about Reiki, thus continuing the connection and education cycle.

We continue to receive inspiring stories. Therefore, if you feel moved and would like to contribute your story involving Reiki, we would be pleased to consider it for our next edition of Reiki Vibes – Heart Warming Stories. Please visit www.reikivibes.com for more information on how to do this.

Be well.

Much love and light,

Tania Bakas and Tracy Lydiatt

Reiki Vibes

May 1, 2009

(Vancouver, Canada & Perth, Australia)

BIOGRAPHIES

Tania Bakas

REIKI REALLY WAS THE LIGHT at the end of the tunnel for me. I had heard of this healing modality a few years before meeting my teacher and Reiki Master, Barb Weston, but my journey was leading me through different experiences at the time.

I attempted to climb the corporate ladder of advertising in Toronto, Ontario and this quest lasted seven years. As my career advanced, my emotional stability declined. A little voice inside me was urging me to make some changes. I took courses in the Aesthetics field. I visualized becoming a home business operator and the idea of self employment became very appealing to me. For the next two years, I worked very hard. I dealt with financial difficulties, debt and daily pressures but most importantly, I fought hard to overcome deep-rooted negative thought patterns. I was on a mission to combat the negative thoughts and emotions that would invade my life and disrupt my harmony. During this quest for self knowledge and healing, I decided to move back to North Vancouver, BC — my hometown. I had once again started from scratch.

Shortly after settling into my new environment, I found Barb Weston. I barely knew how Reiki worked but was intensely drawn to it and was determined to learn about it.

Reflexology also entered my path unexpectedly. I started researching the subject and was very impressed. I felt that this healing modality would be very beneficial to my clients, especially when used in conjunction with Reiki.

Now I am happily self employed and run Giving Within Holistic Healing and have partnered with Tracy Lydiatt on Reiki Vibes. I am so grateful to be here NOW and look forward to healing, helping and sharing the love of Reiki with the rest of the world through Reiki Vibes!

Every day is a learning experience, an opportunity to share and love.

Tracy Lydiatt

I HAVE BEEN PRIVILEGED ENOUGH TO TRAVEL to many places and experience numerous types of educational experiences and healing modalities. Since being introduced to Reiki while in Montana for one summer in 2001, it has begun to seep slowly into my life until it has become a comfortingly quiet pervasive presence in my life.

Reiki is always there for me, providing support and comfort, either through self-sessions, client work or when I'm receiving a

Reiki treatment. I am continually in awe of the clarity, quietness and relaxation it brings into my life.

I am a Sustainability Practitioner and a Reiki Master/Teacher. I enjoy being able to blend my skills and experiences to promote a holistic approach to how we live on the planet. It is my desire through my work and in my personal life to contribute to the healing needs of our bodies as well as the needs of business and community to become better educated in the importance of living holistic, sustainable lives.

I am filled with gratitude everyday for the gift of my life and only hope that my actions with Reiki Vibes will contribute to the health and well-being of those who feel a connection with our mission.